Eye on the Tiger!

He's the hot new player who's taking the world by storm. Here's the story of Tiger Woods, his family, and his future as "the next great golfer." From his multicultural heritage to his record-breaking performances on the golf course, learn how he . . .

- putted on TV with comedian Bob Hope at age two and stole the show;
- won a record three consecutive U.S. Amateur titles and earned *Sports Illustrated*'s Sportsman of the Year for 1996;
- inspired new interest in the sport of golf, bringing new faces to the spectator galleries and becoming a role model to millions of fans;
- became the youngest player ever to win the prestigious Masters Tournament, breaking records for largest win margin and lowest score.

He's Tiger Woods, and he has arrived on the golf scene with a roar.

Books by Bill Gutman

Sports Illustrated: Baseball's Record Breakers
Sports Illustrated: Great Moments in Baseball
Sports Illustrated: Great Moments in Pro Football
Sports Illustrated: Pro Football's Record Breakers
Baseball Super Teams
Bo Jackson: A Biography
Football Super Teams
Grant Hill: A Biography
Great Quarterbacks of the NFL
Great Sports Upsets
Great Sports Upsets 2
Michael Jordan: A Biography
NBA High-Flyers
Pro Sports Champions
Shaquille O'Neal: A Biography
Tiger Woods: A Biography

Available from ARCHWAY Paperbacks

TIGER
WOODS
A BIOGRAPHY

BILL GUTMAN

AN ARCHWAY PAPERBACK
Published by POCKET BOOKS
New York London Toronto Sydney Tokyo Singapore

AN ARCHWAY PAPERBACK *Original*

 An Archway Paperback published by
POCKET BOOKS, a division of Simon & Schuster Inc.
1230 Avenue of the Americas, New York, NY 10020

Copyright © 1997 by Bill Gutman

ISBN: 0-671-88737-8

First Archway Paperback printing July 1997

10 9 8 7 6 5 4 3 2 1

AN ARCHWAY PAPERBACK and colophon are registered trademarks of Simon & Schuster Inc.

Cover photo by J. D. Cubán/Allsport

Printed in the U.S.A.

IL: 7+

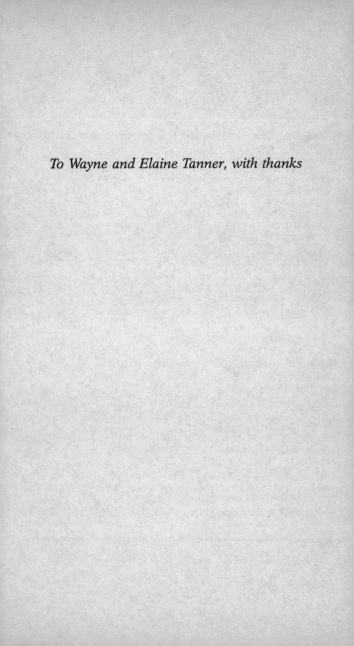

To Wayne and Elaine Tanner, with thanks

Contents

TIGER
WOODS
A BIOGRAPHY

Introduction

The sports world has seen its share of great athletes down through the years. There are stars and there are *superstars*. The true superstars are the men and women who remain at the top of their sport for years, their achievements growing as time passes.

Every once in a while, however, an athlete comes along who is even more than a superstar. He not only plays his sport at the highest level but, with a combination of talent and personality, also alters or changes the face of that sport. This kind of rare athlete is said to transcend his sport, becoming a true celebrity whose name is known throughout the country and, with the instant communication available today, even the world.

These athletes have been exceedingly rare. Babe Ruth, baseball's first home-run king, and Jackie

Robinson, the first African-American to play major league baseball, were two such special athletes. So was Jim Brown, still considered the NFL's all-time greatest running back. He left football while still in his prime to become a movie star.

Bill Russell, Wilt Chamberlain, and Magic Johnson were three NBA giants who not only revolutionized basketball, but were also larger than life personalities. Their legacy is carried on today by Michael Jordan, not only considered the greatest player ever, but probably also the most recognizable and widely known athlete of all time.

Wayne Gretzky in hockey, Jesse Owens in track, Arthur Ashe in tennis, and Muhammad Ali in boxing were four other athletes who managed to transcend their sports by virtue of their personalities, careers, and deeds. There may have been others as well. This is certainly a list open to debate.

The sport of golf has probably had fewer real celebrities than other sports. That doesn't mean there haven't been superstar golfers. There have been many. But golf has produced just two real celebrities—Arnold Palmer and Jack Nicklaus. Both were great golfers who brought new attention and popularity to their sport. Their celebrity, however, came more from their roles as commercial spokesmen and public figures than for their many championships. As golfers, both are now well past their prime.

But suddenly there is a new star on the horizon, one who has soared like a comet in just a few short months. His name is Eldrick Woods, and his nickname is *Tiger*. In August of 1996, Tiger Woods announced, at the tender age of twenty, that he was turning professional and would begin playing on the Pro Golf Tour. By April of 1997, just eight months later, the same Tiger Woods was already being called the best golfer in the world, with a good chance of becoming the greatest of all time. And the nickname *Tiger* was already known throughout the world, perhaps the most recognizable nickname bestowed upon an athlete since the days of Earvin "Magic" Johnson.

How could it happen so quickly, and especially with a golfer? Golf, after all, doesn't normally produce twenty-one-year-old superstars. In fact, it's said that a golfer doesn't reach his prime as a player until his early thirties. That's why Tiger Woods is so special. It isn't only his athletic talent with a golf club, it's the entire package, everything that went into the development of this charismatic new star.

For openers, Tiger is a man of color in a sport that has had very few professionals of African-American or mixed race. His complete heritage is most unusual. His father is half African-American, one-fourth American Indian, and one-fourth Chinese. His mother is half Thai, one-fourth Chinese, and one-fourth Caucasian. That makes Tiger one-fourth African-American, one-fourth Thai, one-fourth Chinese, one-eighth American Indian, and one-eighth Caucasian. Quite a mix. But with the help of his parents, Tiger has made it all work for him.

That brings up the next question. Why did Tiger choose golf? Most youngsters are naturally drawn to the so-called "big three" sports—basketball, football, and baseball. Some, in colder climates, take to ice hockey, maybe snowboarding, or skiing. Others branch out into track and field, a few into tennis, and even fewer to golf. But it wasn't that way with Tiger. His sport was golf from the very beginning, starting shortly after he learned to walk.

It was a love that never wavered. The young Tiger tried the other sports, and was good at them. But each one took time away from golf, and he soon gave them up. Golf was his love, his passion, and even his addiction.

"Golf, to me, is like a drug," Tiger has said many times. "If I don't have it, I go crazy. It's gone beyond love and hate. I always tell people I'm addicted. I've got to keep playing."

Playing, for Tiger Woods, has always meant winning. It started when he was just eight and hasn't stopped. He was an age-group champion, a Junior Amateur Champion, and then U.S. Amateur Champion three straight times. When he turned pro, tour veterans said he was in over his head. Yet he won in just his fifth pro tournament. Then he won a second time, and a third. More and more people began to notice the thin youngster with the winning smile.

But his boyish looks and charm belied an inner toughness second to none. When it was time for the first of golf's four "major" tournaments, the Masters, in April of 1997, critics again said Tiger

Woods wasn't ready to handle the pressure of a major tournament. Yet he proved them wrong once more, not only winning the Masters, but blowing away the field with a record-shattering performance that catapulted him to the top of the sports world.

Now, people can't get enough of Tiger Woods. They want to know everything. How can a rail-thin, six-foot-two, one-hundred-sixty-pound golfer hit a ball farther than anyone else? What gives a twenty-one-year-old nerves of steel on the putting green? How did this young man learn the mental toughness needed to compete and win, often coming from behind to do it?

The answers to these and other questions are quite interesting. For the Tiger Woods story is not about one individual. Rather, it is about a family— a mother, a father, and a son—and how their lives came together for a common purpose. But can Tiger Woods become a true superstar, an athlete who stays on top of his sport for many years? He certainly has the tools to do it, a solid support team, *and* the confidence.

"I know I can handle all this," Tiger has said, "no matter how big it gets. I grew up in the media's eye, but I was taught never to lose sight of where I came from."

Chapter I

Preparing to Raise a Tiger

In most cases, the story of an athlete's life begins with his birth. Tiger Woods was born on December 30, 1975, in Cypress, California. But his story began much earlier than that. The way he was raised had its beginnings long before his birth. It came out of the separate roads traveled by his parents.

Earl Woods didn't have an easy time growing up. When he was just eleven years old, his father died. Right away he lost an important part of his life.

"After the funeral," he remembered, "my mother put her arm around me and said, 'You're the man of the house now.'"

From then on, Earl Woods always had a strong sense of responsibility for others, almost to the point of neglecting himself. He said that he had to look out for everyone else, in effect becoming a father at age eleven. Then, two years later, his mother died. So he was without the parental love and guidance he would later give his own son.

But that wasn't all. Later, Earl Woods attended Kansas State University, where he not only became the first black player on the baseball team, but the first in the entire Big Seven Conference (now called the Big Eight). He was a catcher and a good ballplayer. But in the world of the 1950s, he also experienced something else—the bitter sting of racism.

On road trips he couldn't stay with the team. He often had to travel many miles to find a motel for blacks. And when the team stopped at a restaurant to eat, Earl Woods had to go around to the back door and eat in the kitchen while his teammates sat out front. It wasn't unlike what the early black major league baseball players had to endure at the beginnings of their careers.

But Earl Woods also knew that it wouldn't help to withdraw in his anger and become bitter. Even then, he always vowed to turn negatives into positives, to make whatever happened work for him.

"You don't turn [what happens to you] into hatred," he has said. "You turn it into something positive. Many athletes who reach the top now had things happen to them as children that created hostility, and they bring that hostility with them. But hostility uses up energy. If you can do it without the chip on the shoulder, it frees up all that energy to create."

So Earl Woods slowly learned the lessons he

would later impart to a youthful Tiger. But he was far from over the rough spots of his own life. An early marriage produced three children. But the marriage soon failed, and circumstances caused Earl to lose track of his children for a long time. It was something he always regretted. Perhaps as a result of the things that had happened to him, Earl finally joined the Army.

In the late 1960s, Earl was serving as an Army public information officer in Brooklyn, New York. Decidedly soft duty. But he wanted more. He had himself transferred to the fabled Green Berets, rose to the rank of lieutenant colonel, and served two tours of duty in Vietnam during some of the heaviest fighting of the war. It was while he was serving in Southeast Asia that the final portion of his life which would have a direct bearing on his future son took place.

In Vietnam, Earl formed a close friendship with a South Vietnamese soldier named Nguyen Phong. Phong was such a tenacious soldier and fighter that Earl nicknamed him "Tiger." During his time in Vietnam, Lt. Col. Woods had several close brushes with death. One time a Vietcong sniper bullet hit just alongside one ear, a second bullet just alongside the other. Neither struck him.

Another time, Phong awakened him in the middle of the night and warned him not to move a muscle. A poisonous viper was sitting just inches from his right eye. Phong quickly dispatched the snake. The two men fought side by side, and they saved each other's lives on more than one occasion. But before the war ended, Phong disappeared somewhere in the Vietnamese jungles. Earl Woods never learned whether his friend was dead or alive.

It was also during the war that Earl had occasion to travel to Thailand. At the U.S. Army office in Bangkok he met a Thai woman who was working there as a secretary. Her first name was Kultida, but Earl always simply called her Tida. The two found a common ground. Tida was part Thai and part Chinese, a Buddhist who tried to keep a calmness and serenity about her. Earl was a black American, and Tida knew that there was something smoldering inside him.

"He couldn't relax," she remembered. "He always seemed to be searching for something, never satisfied. I think because both his parents died when he was young, and he didn't have Mom and Dad to make him warm. Sometimes, he stayed awake till three or four in the morning, just thinking."

Tida's life had been far from easy as well. She grew up in a boarding school, after her parents separated when she was just five. Even as a young girl, she vowed that if she ever had a child of her own, he or she would know nothing but love and attention.

After the war, Earl Woods and Tida were married and returned to the United States to live. Earl was still in the Army, but already looking for something else. Finally, the two settled in a one-floor tract house in a middle-class neighborhood in Cypress, California. Soon after that, Tida became pregnant with their first child.

Just a few weeks before Tiger was born there was an incident that reminded both Earl and Tida to keep their guard up. Tida was standing near the kitchen window one night when the house was struck by a number of objects. Someone was shooting BBs and throwing limes at the house. One of the limes shattered the window, spewing pieces of glass all around Tida Woods. Since Earl and Tida were the only non-Caucasian couple in the neighborhood, there was little doubt that the incident was racially motivated.

But nothing could dim the upcoming birth of their child. This was something both parents awaited anxiously. Both of their life experiences had brought them to the point where they planned to devote all their energies to their children. Of course, they didn't know at the time that their first child would be their only one. And that he would certainly be special.

Chapter 2

A Golfing Prodigy

With the birth of their son on December 30, 1975, both Earl and Tida Woods began making good on their vow. Earl nicknamed his son Tiger immediately. And, as with everything else he did in life, he had a good reason. He was naming him after his lost friend in Vietnam.

"I nicknamed him Tiger with the hope that my son would be as courageous as my friend," Earl said. "I also hoped that someday, somehow, Phong would see the names Tiger and Woods together and make the connection."

Unfortunately, that hasn't happened as yet. Earl Woods still doesn't know for sure whether his friend survived the war. But otherwise, the nickname Tiger has served young Eldrick Woods well. It didn't take long for it to become part of his overall identity. That, of course, would go hand in hand with his entry into the world of golf.

That might never have happened, either, if it weren't for Earl Woods' discovery of the game. When he was young, Earl played other sports, but never gave golf much of a thought. And with good reason.

"I was a black kid," he said, "and golf was played at the country clubs. End of story."

In other words, there just weren't many opportunities for poor black youngsters to play golf when Earl Woods was growing up. Many country clubs didn't allow black members then. Clubs were expensive, and not that many kids of *any* kind played the sport at a really early age. The few black golfers in those days learned the game as caddies, carrying the clubs for other golfers and taking a few shots here and there whenever they had the chance.

After returning to the United States following the war, Earl finally decided to take up golf. He first learned the sport from a book, then began playing. Lo and behold, he found he had a real talent for the game. The first time he played he shot a 91 for 17 holes. But he knew he would only play for enjoyment. Not many forty-two-year-olds playing for the first time become pros.

Yet, by the time Tiger was born two years later, Earl had become a fine golfer and had developed a real love for the game. He was practicing constantly. He loved the sport so much that he wanted his son to share it with him.

"I told myself that, somehow, my son would get a chance to play golf early in life."

What neither Earl Woods nor anyone else realized was that it would happen so quickly. When he was just six months old, Tiger would sit in his high chair in the garage and watch his father practice his golf swing. He seemed fascinated by the movement. So it wasn't surprising that soon after he began walking, Tiger began picking up the clubs. He was barely a year old when his father sawed off one of his old clubs to Tiger's size. The boy immediately began trying to copy his father's swing. From that point on, he was hooked on golf.

More amazing than simply being hooked, young Tiger quickly showed real skills. His parents began taking him to the practice green when he was a year old. He already loved putting the ball into the hole. He would jump for joy and squeal with laughter when he made any kind of putt, long or short. Soon, his parents realized their son just couldn't get enough of golf.

"When he was eighteen months old I would take him to the driving range at the Navy Golf Course," Tida Woods said. "And when he was done hitting, I would put him back in the stroller and he'd fall asleep."

As one writer put it, when other toddlers were playing in the sandbox, Tiger was already practicing chipping out of sand. That's how devoted he was to golf before he reached the age of two. It was an incredible beginning to the story, and it wouldn't be long before many more people would know about this golfing phenom from Cypress.

Tiger was just over two years old in 1978 when his mother decided his skills should no longer go unnoticed. She called Los Angeles sportscaster Jim Hill and asked him to come to the Navy Golf Course to see Tiger in action. Hill came out with a film crew and was amazed by what he saw. He had the crew film Tiger playing a complete hole, and when his report aired, he finished with a prediction.

"This young man is going to be to golf what Jimmy Connors and Chris Evert are to tennis."

Connors and Evert, both Americans, were the two reigning stars of tennis in 1978, youngsters who had burst on the scene several years before and rekindled interest in the net game. Both preferred a baseline game as opposed to coming to the net, giving matches longer rallies and somewhat changing the face of the sport. And here was a respected sportscaster like Jim Hill predicting that a two-year-old toddler would someday do the same for golf. It was a brash prediction.

The film clip did draw attention. A short time later, Tiger and his father went on *The Mike Douglas Show*, a popular syndicated talk show of the time. Another guest that day was the legendary comedian, Bob Hope, who was always an avid golfer. Two-year-old Tiger upstaged Hope in a driving contest and on the putting green. It was a great spot, but wouldn't be Tiger's last TV shot. A few years later he would appear on *That's Incredible*, because by age five he was already an incredible golfer. Simple as that.

And by that time his parents were well on their way to making sure that he learned a lot more than golf. If he were to continue along the path to golfing greatness, they knew he would have to be prepared. And that meant becoming a strong, independent, and responsible person first. Then the golfing could follow.

"You have to set your priorities," was the way Earl Woods explained it. "Your priority is the welfare of the child first. Who he is, and what is going into making him a good person, has priority over making him a good athlete. So my time was basically his."

There was always an open-door policy. If Tiger wanted to talk about something, anything, his father would stop what he was doing and talk. As Tiger got older, they would often talk for hours, until each was satisfied. It was something Tiger would never forget, even when he would talk about it in later years.

"Because Dad would always stop to talk with me, it built up a great deal of respect between us. In a sense, a real friendship evolved. He became a counselor, and an advisor, as well as a friend. I'll always love him for it."

That was Earl Woods' motive, building respect and trust.

"The cement that holds all of this together is not love, because love is a given," Mr. Woods explained. "It's respect and trust. Parents figure they don't have to earn diddly from a child. That's not true. Do you think, by right of birth, you are an authoritarian figure from the child's point of view? No! The child did not buy into that situation. He was not consulted. You've got to earn that child's respect and trust, just as he's got to earn yours."

Mr. Woods remembers Tiger asking for a tricycle when he was still a toddler. He asked his son if he *wanted* a tricycle or if he *needed* one.

"Now he has to make a decision," the elder Woods said, "and he'll say, because he's coming from the truth, 'I want it.' Finally, you say okay. But then you know that your son trusts you, and that your word is good."

Mrs. Woods also took part in Tiger's upbringing. She set many of the rules. From the time Tiger was old enough to start school, rule number one was homework first, golf second.

"There was no golf practice until homework was done," Tida Woods said. "Tiger used to tell his friends that his mother was very strict. But he always did his homework first."

Tiger's mother had yet another rule, one that applied once he began playing golf and receiving some notoriety for it. She would absolutely not tolerate temper tantrums. Mrs. Woods made the rule after she noticed Tiger watching tennis players such as Jimmy Connors and John McEnroe, both of whom were known for their emotional outbursts and temper tantrums on the court.

"I would tell him that I didn't want him ruining

my reputation as a parent," she said. "And I promised I would spank him the minute he began acting like that."

By the time Tiger was two, his father had retired from the Army and was working as a purchaser for McDonnell-Douglas. That gave him a nine-to-five job without the concern of being shipped out somewhere. It also provided his family with the stability he felt they deserved. In addition, it gave father and son plenty of time to play golf.

Mr. Woods said that Tiger had already memorized his father's number at work. He would call it often, and always with the same request.

"He would always ask if he could play golf with me today. Each day I would pause, so he would think I might not say yes. Then I would agree, and he would get so excited."

On the golf course there were more lessons to be learned. There were times in the early days when, like most kids, Tiger would bang his club on the ground after hitting a bad shot. Then his father would jump in immediately.

"Who was responsible for that bad shot?" he would ask his son. "Was it the crow who made noise during your backswing? Or was it a bag somebody dropped just as you started to hit? Whose responsibility was the bad shot?"

Tiger would think about it some more and finally answer, "Mine."

That didn't mean the problem was cured immediately. Like any athlete, Tiger would get frustrated when things weren't going well. He would tell his father he couldn't always control his temper, that it just happened, that he was trying very hard.

"I'd tell him I knew he was trying," Mr. Woods explained. "I would also tell him that as he grew and matured, he could turn his anger into an asset, into a desire to do better. And as he grew he would often begin to tell me that he wanted to bang his club on the ground, but instead would say to himself that he was going to hit the next ball real solid.

"He learned to play well even when he was angry because we allowed him the space and then made him take responsibility for his actions. These are just some of the things that apply to all aspects of life that we taught him through golf."

And on the golf course young Tiger's exploits were growing. When he wasn't quite yet three years old, he shot a 48 on the back nine at the Navy Golf Course. He may have been hitting off tees placed closer to the holes, but it was still an amazing exploit. And the lessons continued. One time, when Tiger was four, father and son went to a nearby tournament. Tiger asked his father if he had put his clubs in the trunk of the car.

"I told him that it was his responsibility to remember his own clubs," Mr. Woods recalled. "He was trying to keep from crying, and I told him I was going to practice putting for a while. After about five minutes I came back and said, 'Tiger, I hope you learned your lesson.' I then took his clubs out of the backseat, where I had hidden them. He told me he had learned, and I never had to worry about him taking care of his clubs after that."

The other lesson that Tiger would learn was the inevitable one. That, despite his mixed heritage, he was a black person playing a sport that had always been mostly white. The first evidence of that came at the Navy Golf Course in Cypress, where his father had played—but was not always welcomed with open arms.

"The course was frequented mostly by retired naval personnel," Earl Woods said. "Most of them knew black men only as cooks and servers. Then along comes me, a retired lieutenant colonel who outranked about ninety-nine percent of them. Plus I was a guy who took up golf at the age of forty-two, and I was beating them."

Slowly, Earl Woods began to feel a kind of racism. He was often called Sergeant Brown by other members. The brown referred to the color of his skin, and sergeant because many seemed to feel that was the highest rank that an African-American could ever reach. Finally, a white bartender told the others that Earl had retired as a lieutenant colonel.

"But that wasn't all," Earl said. "I also had the nerve to have this talented kid. So they tried to get to me, through Tiger."

What they did was enforce a long-standing rule that said children under ten could not play the course. This happened when Tiger was three. A year later, there was a new pro at the course. The pro is the man who runs the course, gives instruction, and oversees the entire operation. Earl Woods made a bet with him that Tiger could beat him over nine holes if he spotted Tiger one stroke per hole. If Tiger won, he would be allowed to play the course. Amazingly, the four-year-old won by two strokes, and he was told he could play.

But then the other members intervened. They said once again that Tiger was too young, even though his father repeatedly saw other members' young children playing. This time Earl had seen enough. He walked away from the Navy Golf Course and took Tiger over to the nearby Heartwell Park Golf Club. It was a short, par-3 course in Long Beach. There, the pro, Rudy Duran, wondered if Tiger was good enough to play without getting hurt. Earl had young Tiger begin hitting some shots for him. Duran saw the four-year-old hit just seven shots.

"That was enough," Duran said. "I saw a kid who popped out of the womb a Magic Johnson or a Wolfgang Amadeus Mozart. He had talent oozing out of his fingertips. He was a golfing genius with a natural swing and the ability to learn."

Magic Johnson, of course, was the great point guard for Michigan State and the Los Angeles Lakers. Mozart was a famous composer of classical music who began writing his brilliant music as a young boy. Duran saw Tiger as that same kind of prodigy, and not only cleared him to play, but would also coach him for the next six years.

Chapter 3

A Young Champion

With Rudy Duran becoming part of the team, Tiger learned rapidly. His swing was smooth and natural, his instincts for the game already sharp and true. He kept getting better and better. By the time he was six years old, Duran said he was "like a shrunken touring pro." In fact, he shot his first hole in one when he was just six. No wonder he was so impressive.

When he was just eight he won his first junior world championship, in the ten-and-under division. That meant he beat all the nine- and ten-year-olds. He did it by shooting a 49, 5 under par, in the final round at the par-3 Presidio Hills Golf Course in San Diego. Par for the course was 54.

In a golf tournament, the lowest total score always wins. People who run the course set the pars for each hole. They decide how many strokes a top golfer will need to get the ball from the tee to the hole. They take into account the length of the hole, the distance between *tee* (the starting point) and *green* (where the hole is). If they feel a good golfer should *hole out* (get the ball in the hole) in three strokes, then the *par* is 3. If they feel it should take four or five strokes, then the par is 4 or 5.

If a golfer gets the ball in the hole in three strokes on a par-4 hole, he has scored a *birdie*. If he gets the ball in the hole in two strokes (two under par), it's called an *eagle*. On the other hand, if it takes him five strokes to hole out, he has scored one over par, or a *bogey*. Two over par is a *double-bogey*. And, on the rare occasion with a short hole that a golfer's tee shot reaches the green and rolls into the hole, then he has scored a hole in one or an *ace*. These are some of the golfing terms that Tiger learned as a young boy.

Most golf courses consist of eighteen holes. To play all eighteen is called a *round*. If the par for the entire course is, say, seventy strokes, or a 70, then a golfer shooting below 70 is breaking par for the round. If it takes more than seventy strokes, he is over par. Most tournaments consist of four rounds, or seventy-two holes. The lowest total score for the seventy-two holes wins. A few tournaments are five rounds, with a total of ninety holes. This kind of golf is called *medal play*. There can be many players, but only one winner.

There is one other kind of tournament. It's called *match play*, where one golfer goes up against another. The winner is the one who has the lowest score for the most holes. Total score doesn't count. So, if one golfer takes three strokes to get the ball in the hole and the other takes four, the golfer with the 3 has won the hole. He is now 1 up on the day. The match ends when one player has won so many holes that his opponent can't catch him. So if a player wins 3-and-2, that means he had a three hole lead with only two holes remaining. The opponent can't win.

It was after Tiger's first junior title at Presidio that Earl Woods realized for the first time just how competitive his son had become. Whenever the two would practice and play together, Tiger was always talking about his score, how he wanted it to be lower and lower. Finally, Mr. Woods told his son to stop worrying about his score and just start enjoying himself. The reply he got surprised him.

"That's how I enjoy myself," Tiger said. "Shooting low numbers makes me happy."

Mr. Woods thought about his son's answer for a minute, then realized what it meant.

"That day changed our relationship," he said. "I told him I would never again be on his case for being obsessed with his score. After that I began establishing special pars for him. I would give him two extra shots per hole. So if the par for a hole was 4, Tiger's par would be 6. I didn't want Tiger to feel he couldn't compete. If I expected him to shoot adult pars at age nine, it would have been totally unrealistic and I'd be a stupid parent."

By this time Tiger was already talking about becoming a professional golfer someday and winning all the big tournaments. He simply loved to win. When he was ten years old, veteran pro John Anselmo took over as Tiger's coach. He would guide the young star until he was seventeen and ready for college. But Earl Woods was never far from the scene. And there was still one aspect of his son's training that Earl took care of in his own special way.

Using part of his Green Beret training as a guide, Mr. Woods decided he would be the one to create an unshakable mental toughness in his son. You can have all the natural skills in the world, but if you don't have the mental toughness to perform under intense pressure, you won't win. So when the two went out to play, Earl told Tiger he was going to do all kinds of things to rattle him, almost taking him to the breaking point.

"I pulled every nasty, dirty, obnoxious trick on him, week after week," Mr. Wood admitted.

That included dropping a bag of clubs just before the impact of Tiger's swing. Imitating the sound of a bird or other animal just as Tiger was getting ready to putt. He would sometimes toss a ball right in front of Tiger's line of vision just as he was getting ready to hit. He would stand in his line of sight and then move just as he was about to hit his shot. He would cough, rattle keys, play mind games by telling him he better not hit the ball into the water when they were near a water hazard.

Sometimes Tiger would become so exasperated that he would stop his swing and glare at his father, who would then bark, "Don't look at me. Are you gonna hit the ball or not?"

Tiger would later admit this was one of the most difficult experiences of his life. The two had a code word. If Tiger had enough, all he had to do was say the code word and his father would stop. Never once, according to Earl Woods, did Tiger so much as utter the code word.

"I taught him every trick an opponent could possibly pull, and some I invented myself," Mr. Woods said. "I'm not really proud of this, but I even cheated, just to get a reaction from him. Let's face it. Somewhere down the line somebody was going to do that, too. I made sure he was exposed to every devious, diabolical, insidious trick. It was a very difficult thing for me to do, and it didn't really fill me with pride and joy. But if he was going to continue in golf, I felt it was necessary."

This kind of radical training worked because of the love and trust between a father and son.

"He knew I wouldn't do anything to hurt him," Mr. Woods said. "At the end, I told him I'd never met another person as mentally tough as he was."

The confidence Tiger gained from these often difficult sessions came through later. Once Tiger began to really compete on the national level—as an amateur, a collegian, and then a pro—his mental toughness always amazed his coaches, opponents, and those watching. Asked about it, he would simply say, with conviction: "I *am* the toughest golfer mentally." Period.

To someone who didn't know Earl or Tiger, it

might appear that young Tiger was being pushed, being forced to become the best golfer he could be at too young an age. The sports world has been filled with teenage phenoms who burn out or rebel, and parents who push too hard, hoping their offspring can achieve something they could never achieve. Or they simply push their kids, hoping they will become a cash cow for the entire family. The huge amounts of money waiting for sports stars can be tempting. It can reward, but it can also corrupt.

This simply was never the case with Earl and Tiger. All those who knew the family were aware that it was simply a matter of two best friends working together toward a mutually agreed-upon goal.

"Many people thought Earl Woods was just another dominating stage father," was the way one writer put it. "But Tiger took to the game. Earl never had to tell him to practice. In fact, his parents had to pull him back a little."

There was even more evidence of this as the years passed. Tiger and his father often played golf with a man named Jay Brunza, who was a retired captain in the Navy Medical Service Corps. When Tiger was fourteen, his father asked Brunza to take on the role of sports psychologist for Tiger. He would work on helping Tiger to relax, to focus, and to manage his anger. Brunza spent a great deal of time with both father and son. He observed the full family relationship, and his conclusion was that it was an extremely healthy one.

"Tiger was pursuing something from an intrinsic passion for the game, and wasn't forced to live out somebody else's expectations," Brunza said. "If he said, 'I'm tired of golf, I want to collect stamps,' his parents would say, 'Fine, son,' and walk him down to the post office."

As Tiger would say later, golf was always an addiction for him, a sport he simply loved from the first and never stopped loving. During his teen years he tried all the other sports and was quite good at them. When he played baseball, he was a natural switch-hitter. On the basketball court, his favorite position was shooting guard. And, as they say on the playground, he could drain the "J." His speed and agility made him a fine wide receiver in football, and when he went out on the track he was a swift 400-meter runner.

Had Tiger decided to concentrate on these other sports, he surely might have been good enough to become a professional in one or more of them. But, as with everything else, those sports had to take a backseat to golf. One by one he simply gave them up, stopped playing. They all interfered with his time at the golf course, or at the driving range, or putting green. Golf, simply put, was everything. And he was beginning to reap the rewards of his perseverance.

By the time he was fourteen, Tiger had already won five age-group junior world titles. That was two more than any other golfer had ever won. But winning more than anyone else would become a habit. He had also won more than 100 local junior titles, and there was barely enough room in the Woods household for all the trophies he brought home. Even then his reputation was spreading, and his talent was scaring competitors.

His friend, fellow golfer Notah Begay, explained how it was in those days.

"The other guys knew I was Tiger's friend," Begay said, "Before a tournament they would always ask me if Tiger was really as good as people said he was. So he had already taken on a celebrity status and most of the other guys were afraid of him [on the golf course]."

So the legend was already growing. In August of 1990, Tiger played a round with twenty-one touring pros at the Insurance Youth Golf Classic, a pro junior event in Fort Worth, Texas. Playing with nerves of steel and with that mental toughness he had learned, Tiger finished the eighteen holes with a score of 69. It was good enough to beat eighteen of the twenty-one pros who also shot that day.

All of them were amazed by the tall, thin youngster who could already hit the ball a country mile. One of them, Tommy Moore, put it this way.

"I wish I could have played like that at fourteen," Moore said, then added quickly, "Heck, I wish I could play like that at twenty-seven."

In the fall of 1990, Tiger entered Western High School in Anaheim as a ninth-grader, a freshman. His skills on the golf course were already known throughout California, and letters from colleges were already starting to arrive at the Woods's home, even though college was still four years away. In fact, Tiger had gotten his first prerecruiting letter from Stanford University when he was just thirteen.

It wasn't so farfetched when you consider that this high school freshman had beaten eighteen of twenty-one pro golfers in a round the year before. Already tall at five-feet-eleven, but thin at 138 pounds, Tiger was already thinking about the pros.

"I plan to get my [college] degree first, and then tear up the [Pro] Tour," he said.

That, too, wasn't so farfetched. John Anselmo, who had coached Tiger since he was ten, couldn't help but look ahead.

"With Tiger, anything is possible," said the sixty-nine-year-old coach. "I kid his dad that Tiger is not his, but that he comes from another world. I just hope I live long enough to see what's going to happen. It's going to be amazing."

Tiger himself was already aware that there had been very few African-American golfers on the Pro Tour. He also knew that, as of 1991, it had been five years since a black golfer had won a Tour event. He had heard whisperings that he could become the best black golfer on the Tour someday. But that wasn't how he saw himself.

"I don't want to be the best *black* golfer on the Tour," he said, self-assuredly. "I want to be the best golfer on the Tour."

In February of 1991, Tiger was playing a very important round at the Los Serranos Country Club in Chino, California. There were 132 golfers entered, and two of them would qualify to play in the

Nissan Los Angeles Open the following week. It was a Professional Golf Association (PGA) Tour event. If Tiger qualified, he would become the youngest golfer ever to play in a PGA tournament.

On the first four holes Tiger looked much like a nervous kid who was in over his head. He hit a tree from the rough, and put two other tee shots off the fairway onto cart paths. But after that he suddenly began to play like a seasoned veteran. He sank two fifteen-foot birdie putts, one on the sixth hole and another on the seventh. Then on the eighth he chipped the ball in the cup from forty yards away for a two-under-par eagle.

"Don't touch me, I'm burning up," he told his father, meaning he was playing great golf.

He continued to stay in contention. Then, on the sixteenth hole, he amazed everyone watching with a drive that carried an incredible 344 yards. It was a 504-yard hole. He then pitched onto the green and two-putted for yet another birdie. But it was his mammoth drive that caught everyone's eye. There are pro golfers who never hit the ball that far.

Seeing Tiger hit, Ron Hinds, who was the pro at the Westlake Village Golf Course, would say later, "You try to avoid envy in golf, but that kid humbled all of us."

It finally came down to the eighteenth and last hole. Veteran pro Mac O'Grady had already finished at eight under par for the round. And Tiger's father heard that someone else had come in at seven under. Going into the final hole, Tiger was at six under par. Tiger had already hit his tee shot on the par-5 hole when his father told him he needed a birdie on the hole to tie for second. He figured his second shot would have to travel 250 yards to clear the pond in front of the green, and another 30 yards to reach the green in two shots. That would give him a chance for an eagle.

Perhaps Tiger simply tried too hard. He didn't want to play short. But in trying to drive all the way to the green he mis-hit the ball. It landed smack in the pond. Tiger had to take a penalty stroke and wound up with a six for the hole. It was his only bogey of the day. His final score of 69 was good, but not good enough to qualify him for the Nissan L.A. Open. It was a bitter disappointment, and he felt he had let everyone down. Those around him, however, knew there would be other days.

"Tiger won't lose his motivation," said Jay Brunza. "His motivation comes from within. That's why I don't see him burning out. Golf is simply pure pleasure for him."

And Ron Hinds, who marveled at Tiger's mammoth drive on sixteen, said he was hoping Tiger qualified.

"I honestly felt myself rooting for him," Hinds said. "I was hoping he would get into the tournament so I could watch this awesome kid play against [Tom] Kite and [Ben] Crenshaw and those guys. After seeing Tiger play, you can't help but wonder what might have been."

Kite and Crenshaw were just two of the top pros

on the tour. And here was Ron Hinds, just one of many who already felt fifteen-year-old Tiger Woods could compete with them. It wouldn't be that long before he could.

Tiger continued to grow and show a maturity beyond his years. The trust fostered between Tiger and his parents showed itself in many ways. He was still fifteen when he traveled to New Orleans with his father to play in yet another amateur tournament. One evening, he asked if he could go into town with some of the other players. Mr. Woods gave him twenty dollars and told him to have fun . . . but to get back at a reasonable hour. Tiger told him he'd be back by 11 P.M.

At 10:50 P.M., Tiger came walking to his father's room, excited by the sights and sounds of downtown New Orleans. Then Mr. Woods asked where his friends were. Tiger admitted they were drinking alcohol, while he stuck to cherry soda. The other boys stayed out beyond the tournament curfew and were disqualified.

"Tiger learned at a very early age to live by the rules," his father said. "There are always rules in life. If you don't believe it, break them, and you will come into contact with the enforcement element in our society."

That was something Tiger wasn't about to do. He already knew what he wanted. In fact, a year later, at age sixteen, he did become the youngest player ever to make it into a PGA Tournament. He was moving forward right on schedule.

Chapter 4

The Titles Start to Come

In the summer of 1991, Tiger stepped onto the national stage for the first time. Though just a freshman in high school, he won the first of his U.S. Junior Amateur Championships. By that time, his routine was established. Schoolwork still came first. He was an outstanding student at Western High for four years. And, as always, after studying came golf.

Playing since the age of one, Tiger was already fundamentally sound in every aspect of the game. His natural swing generated incredible power. His mental toughness served his short game well. Now it was just a matter of experience and a matter of time. It didn't seem as if anything could slow his rise to the top.

He won a second straight U.S. Junior Amateur title in 1992, and also played (as an amateur) in his first pro event. At year's end he was cited as the nation's top amateur player by *Golf Digest*, *Golf-Week*, and *Golf World*. He was still only sixteen.

A year later he took an unprecedented third U.S. Junior title. No other player had ever won more than one. He also played in three PGA Tour events as an amateur. Though he didn't come close to winning, failing to make the cut (having a score low enough to continue to the final 36 holes) in each, he nevertheless picked up valuable experience and began getting a feel for the pro game.

The following year, 1994, having just graduated from Western High, Tiger was playing for the United States Amateur title. At the age of eighteen he was going up against amateur golfers of all ages. It would be his toughest test yet.

Tiger had already accepted a scholarship offer from Stanford University and would be going to that California school in the fall. However, there were clamorings being heard about him turning pro. He still insisted that he wanted his education first. Then he would undoubtedly hit the Pro Tour. But first things first. And that was the U.S. Amateur.

The United States Amateur Championship is a unique kind of tournament. All the entrants begin by playing two rounds of medal play, thirty-six holes. After those two rounds, the lowest scoring sixty-four players qualify for match play. Then they must go up against one another in eighteen-hole matches. The loser is eliminated, the winner moves on. Finally, the two finalists play thirty-six holes of match play to determine the champion.

Playing his usual all-around game, Tiger ripped through the two rounds of medal play and easily qualified to go on to match play. There he moved ahead, winning five matches to propel himself into the final against a golfer named Trip Kuehne. Tiger was the favorite, but for nearly the first half of the match it looked more like Trip Kuehne was going to become the champion. After thirteen holes of the championship, Kuehne already had a substantial, six-hole lead over Tiger.

But then Tiger did something that would become his trademark over the next several years and make him the most feared player in the game. He turned it up a notch and began playing great golf, making one tough shot after another. Kuehne's lead began to disappear. By the time they reached the final holes, it was apparent that Tiger would become the youngest U.S. Amateur Champion in history.

When it ended, Tiger went over and gave his father a long hug. There were tears in the eyes of both men. The vision that both had was beginning to come true. Now it would be a matter of Tiger balancing everything—school, golf, family—and making it all work.

That fall, Tiger started his freshman year at Stanford. He would play golf for Coach Wally Goodwin, and decided he would study economics. As he had always been in the past, Tiger was a fine student, making sure his schoolwork was done before he would go to the golf course or party with his schoolmates.

Though studies and golf came first, Tiger also gained from the experience of meeting new friends, people from all parts of the country. He loved to sit up half the night talking to them about various aspects of life. He had friends of all colors and nationalities, and the subject of race came up quite often, the undergrads all swapping stories.

Tiger talked about his first day at kindergarten years earlier. He was grabbed by a gang of older kids who tied him to a tree, then threw rocks at him while calling him names like "monkey" and "nigger." It was a horrible experience for a five-year-old, so much so that he didn't even tell his parents what happened for several days.

Living in California, most of the instances of racism were more subtle than that first one, but they certainly occurred from time to time. His father's experience at the Navy Golf Course, when Tiger was banned for being too young, was one example. There was a much more recent incident, when Tiger was at a driving range near the family home hitting his huge drives into the protective netting that shielded nearby homes. Someone called the police to complain that a black teenager was trying to bombard his house.

The discussions at Stanford became more intense when Tiger and some of his friends took a course in African-American history. He related to his friends the looks he and his father would get over the years in various country club locker rooms and restaurants.

"It's something a white person could never understand," Tiger said, "unless he went to Africa and suddenly found himself in the middle of a tribe."

Through his studies and discussions with friends, Tiger came to yet another conclusion.

"What I realized," he said, "is that even though I'm mathematically Asian—if anything—if you have one drop of black blood in the United States, you're black. And how important it is for this country to talk about the subject."

At that point, Tiger wasn't in a position to talk publicly about race. How he dealt with the subject would be something he would have to decide on in later years. But he did tell his friends about another aspect of his life, something many African-Americans didn't share. That was his mother's Buddhist religion. Every so often he would accompany his mother to a Buddhist temple and participate in some of the rituals. In many ways, he found the religion, and Asian culture, very comforting.

"I like Buddhism because it's a whole way of being and living," he explained. "It's based on discipline and respect and personal responsibility. I like the Asian culture better than ours because of that. Asians are much more disciplined than we are. Look how well-behaved their children are. It's how my mother raised me. You can question, but talk back? Never. In Thailand, once you've earned people's respect, you have it for life. Here, it's, 'what have you done for me lately?' So here you can never rest easy. In this country I have to be very careful. I'm easygoing, but I won't let you in completely."

So, while he didn't talk about it very often, Tiger thought about things very deeply and kept his guard up. He also knew that the more tournaments he won, the more famous he became, the harder it would be. But he also felt that the upbringing given him by his parents would allow him to handle most anything that came his way.

Tiger enjoyed his freshman year at Stanford. He played outstanding golf for the school team and continued his tournament play whenever he had the chance. That summer he picked up some valuable experience by playing in the Master's Championship, where he was the low amateur, and later in both the Scottish and British Opens. He was learning that there was more to making a great golf shot than just overpowering the ball or hitting it on a straight line to the hole.

"When Tiger plays with guys like [Fred] Couples, [Greg] Norman, [Nick] Faldo, and [Nick] Price, he marvels at the way they control the ball in the air," said his new coach, Butch Harmon. "After the British Open he asked me how far away he was from being at their level. 'When will I be that good?' was the way he put it. I told him he just had to keep working. 'You've got so much to learn,' I said. He knows it and is willing to keep working."

Couples, Norman, Faldo, and Price were four of the best touring professionals on the circuit. Like all great champions, Tiger wanted to learn by watching the best. They were the barometer by which he measured himself. And those guys, in turn, probably knew that this thin kid would be competing with them in the not-too-distant future.

Then in late August, just before the start of his sophomore year at Stanford, Tiger traveled to the Newport Country Club in Newport, Rhode Island, to defend his United States Amateur Championship. Once again he ripped through the two rounds of medal play and into the match-play phase of the tournament.

In the semifinals he had a tough match with a forty-three-year-old named Mark Plummer, who was an eight-time Maine Amateur champ and two-time New England Amateur titleholder. Plummer kept it close all the way. Tiger didn't wrap it up until the eighteenth and final hole. But he won and returned for the thirty-six-hole final.

This time he was up against George "Buddy" Marucci, another forty-three-year-old who had never advanced past the second round in any previous U.S. Amateur. But Marucci was playing great golf this week and started out as if he intended to teach the teenage Tiger a lesson. After twelve holes, Marucci had a three-hole lead, and when they turned the corner at nineteen, he was still 2-up.

Marucci continued to play well. During one stretch late in the round he had three birdies over a four-hole span. But by then Tiger had turned it up a notch and was closing the gap. Then, he finally took over the lead. Going into the thirty-sixth and final hole, Tiger was 1-up. All he had to do was win or halve (tie) the hole, and the title was his.

It finally came down to this. Marucci was already on the green with a chance for a twenty-foot birdie putt. Tiger was still about 140 yards out. If he didn't make a good shot and put the ball near the hole, Marucci would have a good chance to draw even and put the match into sudden death. Tiger took an eight iron from his bag and prepared to hit. Announcing the match for ESPN was former pro Johnny Miller. Watching Tiger get ready to hit, Miller said,

"I wouldn't be surprised if he knocks it a foot from the hole."

Tiger took that perfect swing of his and hit a high, arcing shot that flew right over the flag (which sits in the hole to mark where it is), then spun back, rolling to within inches of the cup. It was a brilliant shot, and the gallery erupted in jubilant applause. Seconds later, Tiger holed his putt and punched the air in triumph. He had won a second straight U.S. Amateur and was very pleased with his effort.

"This one means more [than the first] because it showed how far my game has come," Tiger said. "That shot at eighteen. That's the only shot I could hit close, that half shot. I didn't have it last year and I didn't have it at [the Masters] Augusta."

Runner-up Buddy Marucci was also extremely impressed with the play of young Tiger Woods.

"Tiger's the best athlete that this [level] of golf has seen," Marucci said. "He's lean, he's strong, his swing is marvelous. I couldn't see the ball come off the club for the first twenty-seven holes. It came off the club that fast."

For Jay Brunza it was even more than that. "Tiger has the ability to raise his game when he has to," Brunza said.

That's an ability that only the truly great ones have—athletes like Michael Jordan, Magic Johnson, Joe Montana—guys who play their very best when everything is on the line. Tiger was showing that ability more and more as he matured.

Then in the happy celebration that followed, Earl Woods felt it was time to make a bold prediction about his son.

"Before Tiger is through," the elder Woods said, "he is going to win fourteen major championships."

Chapter 5

A Third Amateur and an Exciting Debut

Shortly after his triumph at Newport, Tiger returned to Stanford for his sophomore year. He settled back into the routine of campus life and seemed happy. In fact, he was. Tiger enjoyed learning and studying, had good friends, and was the top player on the Stanford golf team. That should have been more than enough for someone still a couple of months away from his twentieth birthday.

But there was something else, something that had been with him for nearly all of his twenty years. That was the absolute lure of the links (a term for the golf course), of golf. It was getting to the point where Tiger knew he could compete with almost anyone. How much longer would he be content to play against college teams and amateurs who only played on weekends or vacations?

He'd already had a taste of pro tournaments, seen the atmosphere at Augusta during Masters week and at St. Andrews for the British Open.

He also heard the things the pros were saying about him. Like any great athlete, there was the desire to test himself against the very best. In addition to all that, there was also some good money to be made as a professional golfer. His father had left his job at McDonnell-Douglas back in 1988 to work with Tiger full-time. With everything else, there had to be the thought of earning enough money to make his parents' lives a bit easier.

There was still another factor, one which Tiger was also well aware of, and that was the role of the black man in professional golf. There were precious few, and as of late 1995, only one African-American on the pro tour. That was Jim Thorpe, who had won a number of tournaments in the 1980s and was a good, solid golfer. But he wasn't considered among the golfing elite and was just a few years away from being eligible for the senior tour, open to golfers age fifty and over.

To fully appreciate the things Tiger had to think about, it's necessary to review briefly the history of the sport. Golf originated in Scotland several hundred years ago. The first formal golf club was established in Edinburgh, Scotland, way back in 1744. There were already forms of the game being played in the United States, but the first real club and course was the Saint Andrew's Golf Club of Yonkers, New York, established in 1888.

Of the major tournaments, the British Open is the oldest, having been played for the first time back in 1860. The United States Open was held for the first time in 1895. So the tournament is now more than 100 years old. The Masters was played for the first time in 1934, while the PGA Championship began back in 1916.

It is estimated that there are some twenty million golfers in the United States today with more than 8,000 professionals. Yet, for several reasons, the sport has never been one to attract many minorities. One reason is that golf has often been played at country clubs, many of which restricted their membership for years. African-Americans, as well as people of Spanish or Asian ancestry, just weren't welcomed.

In addition, many minority populations were concentrated in urban areas, and there aren't too many golf courses located in the middle of a large city. Places to play were simply not there. The few blacks who pursued the sport to the point of becoming pros learned the game while caddying (carrying bags of clubs) for golfers at country clubs or perhaps municipal courses. These pioneers simply found they enjoyed the game and eventually found a way to play and improve. But the number of black players who earned respect and some victories on the pro tour could be counted on the fingers of one hand.

There was Charlie Sifford, now seventy-four, who joined the PGA Tour in 1960. Sifford was really the first to show that an African-American could compete on the Pro Tour. He was the oldest player to earn an exemption from the prior year's money list when he finished in the top twenty-eight in 1986 at the age of sixty-four. Sifford also won six Negro National Open titles, and was honored as one of the top 100 people in the First Century of Golf.

Lee Elder will always have a special place in golf's history. Now sixty-two, Elder joined the PGA tour in 1967 and has won more than $1 million in career earnings. In 1975 he became the first African-American to compete in the Masters Tournament in Augusta, Georgia. He has four PGA Tour titles, with three of them coming in 1985. The first came in 1974, which made him eligible for the Masters. He now competes on the Senior Tour.

Jim Dent joined the PGA Tour in 1970 and moved on to the Senior Tour in 1989. Since that time he has won ten Senior titles and is approaching $5 million in prize money for his career. If he makes it, he will be just the ninth golfer to reach that dollar mark. In 1994, Dent won $950,891 with his Senior Tour play, showing that the fifty-seven-year-old is one of the finest senior golfers on the circuit.

Calvin Peete, now fifty-three, joined the PGA tour in 1975 and moved on to the Senior Tour in 1993. Peete has also had a very successful career, with twelve PGA Tour victories, beginning with the Greater Milwaukee Open in 1979. Unlike Tiger, who began to play as soon as he was able to walk, Calvin Peete didn't learn the sport until he was twenty-three. But he has racked up some $2.3

million in prize money and as of early 1996 was the last African-American to win a PGA Tour event.

Many young African-American athletes playing professional baseball, football, and basketball today have been criticized for knowing very little about the history of their sport, especially about the contributions made by older African-Americans, the pioneer players who helped make it possible for today's athletes to make millions of dollars. This simply was not the case with Tiger Woods.

Tiger had studied the history of golf, had been told about the way it was by his father and others who had come before. He was very familiar with names like Sifford, Elder, Dent, Peete and Thorpe. He already knew that when he turned pro he could be continuing a legacy they had started and would be carrying the banner for all of them. It was still another burden he would have to carry on his shoulders.

So these were all factors when the second semester of his sophomore year began early in 1996. Then, before the school year ended, Tiger won the NCAA championship. He was now the best golfer in the college ranks and would soon be named College Player of the Year. He had reached yet another of his goals.

That summer, he once again traveled across the Atlantic to compete in the British Open as an amateur. In the second round of that prestigious old tournament, Tiger Woods suddenly caught fire. He was playing with verve and daring, his drives bringing *ooohs* and *aaaahs* from the gallery and his short game full of confidence. When the round ended, Tiger had shot an amazing 66, and was up among the leaders of the tournament.

He faltered somewhat in the final two rounds, finishing in a tie for twenty-second. But it was still his best finish in a pro event, and a major, at that. Yet it was his 66 that he remembered.

"Something really clicked that day," he said, "like I had found a whole new style of playing. I finally understood the meaning of playing within myself. Ever since, the game has seemed a lot easier."

The tournament, and especially that 66, made Tiger think even more about turning pro. He began talking with his parents and a few trusted advisors about the possibility. He reminded his parents of his promise to finish school and get his degree. He told them no matter what happened, he would honor that promise.

"You can get your degree now or you can get it twenty years from now," his father told him.

There were also strong indications by this time that when Tiger turned pro, there would be a number of major endorsement deals opening up for him. Companies felt he had the kind of charisma that would make him a very marketable athlete, if he chose to go that route. So there was the the obvious possibility of a great deal of money coming Tiger's way. Of course, for all that to happen, he would have to continue to play winning golf.

His next big test would be the U.S. Amateur Championship at the end of August. No golfer had ever won this event three years in a row. With two titles already in the bag, Tiger was poised to make amateur golf history. It began to look as if the decision about turning pro would be made prior to or immediately after the U.S. Amateur.

With all that on his mind, Tiger entered the Western Amateur, which was held about a month before the U.S. Amateur, and he didn't play well. It was a match play tournament and Tiger was beaten in the first round by nineteen-year-old Terry Noe, the 1994 Junior champion.

"I was just flat, and that told me something," Tiger said after his defeat.

What it told him was that he was simply juggling too many things at once. School would be starting again. There was pressure to defend his U.S. Amateur title, and pressure about turning professional. He knew he would have to make a decision and put his life on a single track.

During the month between the Western Amateur and the U.S. Amateur there was a great deal of behind-the-scenes activity in the Woods camp. Tiger spoke to a number of touring pros—Fred Couples, Curtis Strange, Greg Norman and Ernie Els—asking each if they thought he should turn pro. All agreed that he was ready both mentally and physically to go out on the Tour.

Once Earl Woods saw that his son was serious about turning pro, he also went to work, getting people to look into the other side of being a pro.

He quickly found that Tiger was looked upon as an athlete with tremendous endorsement potential. Once various companies learned that Tiger Woods might be available, a huge bidding war ensued, the likes of which had never occurred before over a young golfer. So the tension was building and the public continued to wonder what the charismatic youngster would do.

When he arrived at the Pumpkin Ridge course near Portland, Oregon, everyone was trying to guess what he would do. Tiger and his camp remained quiet. A week after the Amateur, the pros would be gathering in Wisconsin for the Greater Milwaukee Open. There was conjecture that Tiger would turn pro right after the Amateur tournament, then head to Milwaukee for his pro debut the following week. It was the main topic of conversation as the U.S. Amateur tourney got under way. The trick for Tiger would be to maintain his concentration on golf. The fact that Tiger was trying to become the first to win three straight, as well as the question of his turning pro, made the 1996 United States Amateur the most attended and watched ever.

Whenever a reporter or even a fan would ask him if he was about to turn pro, Tiger would simply say, "In the future. I can't afford to think about it now. I know from experience that that just causes anxiousness."

In other words, he knew he had to concentrate on the tournament. Those watching would sure get their money's worth. Showing almost no signs of pressure, Tiger played excellent golf throughout the two medal rounds. His 69-67—136 was the lowest score among the 312 golfers in the field. But it was far from over. Now the top sixty-four had to engage in single-elimination match play. Tiger won his first matches quite easily. But then came the eighteen-hole semifinal match against Tiger's Stanford teammate, Joe Kribel.

At first, Tiger seemed to falter. Kribel went 2-up after just four holes as the huge galleries tried to urge Tiger to rally. At the tenth hole Tiger was on the brink of going 3-down when he made a brilliant shot out of a sand trap and recovered to halve the hole. He was still 2-down, but suddenly his confidence was growing. And though he was just a twenty-year-old amateur, Tiger already had a reputation of making up strokes with lightning efficiency.

Tiger made two quick birdies and then an eagle on the back nine, while Kribel became unnerved and faltered. The defending champ quickly took the lead and closed out the match on the seventeenth hole, winning 3 and 1. That meant he had gone three strokes up with just one hole remaining. Now just thirty-six holes of match play remained between Tiger and a third straight championship—and maybe a huge announcement.

"All I have to do is stay strong up here," Tiger said, pointing to his head with a finger.

Mental toughness. All those hard lessons from his father. He would need every inch of it in a heart-stopping final against another brash young golfer, nineteen-year-old Steve Scott, who was preparing to enter his sophomore year at the University of Florida. So the question was, would one young golfing sensation be upset by another?

Once again, Tiger seemed to follow a familiar pattern. He didn't start strong, and Scott took advantage of the defending champ's shoddy play. His confidence growing, Scott charged to a four-hole lead after the first nine holes. With nearly 15,000 fans crowding the course at each hole, the match continued. Tiger began playing better, but Scott refused to fold.

After twenty holes and with just sixteen left to play, Scott had increased his lead to five holes. Once again it would take a furious Woods comeback to retain his title. Tiger took a deep breath, gathered himself, and went to work. Beginning with the twenty-first, he won three straight holes, pulling within two. He got it down to a single hole before Scott made a spectacular shot on the twenty-eight to go 2-up once again. Now there were just eight holes left.

Then, on the 553-yard, par-5, twenty-ninth hole, Tiger once again amazed everyone. His drive carried some 350 feet off the tee. Then he took a five iron and drove the ball onto the green, some forty-five feet from the hole. Still not finished, he rolled in a long, curving eagle putt to take the hole from Scott, who also played it well for a birdie. Yet Scott would still not yield. He rallied again and with just three holes left, Tiger was 2-down. If Scott won the thirty-fourth hole, the match would be over.

With the championship on the line with every shot, Tiger holed an eight-foot birdie putt to win the hole. Then on the thirty-fifth hole, Tiger pushed his approach shot to the green some thirty-five feet from the cup. Once again the pressure was on. And once again Tiger came through. He rolled the long putt into the cup to win the hole and draw even with Scott for the first time. He punctuated his long putt by thrusting his fist in the air.

"That's a feeling I'll remember for the rest of my life," Tiger said later, referring to the clutch putt.

Now the two went to the thirty-sixth and final hole, with each having a chance to win. But when they halved the hole, it was time for the match to go into sudden death. First player to win a hole would take the title.

The two golfers continued the dogfight. They halved the thirty-seventh hole of the championship, but Scott had a chance to win. He missed an eighteen-foot putt that would have given him the championship. Now they moved to the thirty-eighth, which was the 194-yard, par-3, tenth hole on the course.

Tiger hit a beautiful 6 iron from the tee, dropping the ball just twelve-feet from the pin. Then Scott faltered. His tee shot went into the rough. He needed a second shot to reach the green, the ball resting eleven feet from the hole. Tiger's putt for birdie came within eighteen inches of the cup. But when Scott missed his putt for par, Tiger only had to sink the eighteen-incher to win.

He lined it up carefully, stood over the ball for a few seconds as the huge gallery fell silent. Then he stroked the ball firmly. It rolled in! The crowd erupted in wild cheers as Tiger again thrust his fist into the air. He had done it. He had won a third straight United States Amateur Championship. After a brief celebration on the green, Tiger followed his usual postmatch ritual. He gave big bear hugs to both his mother and father.

"All I kept telling myself down the stretch was that I've been here before," Tiger said. "The fortunate part was I had thirty-six holes."

Even runner-up Scott knew he had been part of history. "That was probably the best Amateur final match ever," he said. "Just to be part of it, I feel completely a winner."

By Sunday night, the cat was out of the bag. Tiger was completely drained by the week's 156 holes of pressure-packed golf. He just showered and ate a pizza at a friend's house in Portland where his family was staying. It had already been announced that he would hold a news conference the following Wednesday, the day before the Greater Milwaukee Open. Tiger finally admitted what everyone just about knew for sure.

"I had intended to stay in school, play four years at Stanford, and get my degree," he told a reporter. "But things change. I didn't know my game was going to progress to this point. It became harder to get motivated for college matches, and since I accomplished my goal of winning the NCAA, it was going to get harder still. Finally, winning the third Amateur in a row is a great way to go out. I always said I would know when it was time. Now is the time."

The official announcement came on Wednesday, August 28, 1996. As expected, Tiger Woods told the world he was leaving Stanford University and would join the PGA Tour. At the age of twenty, he was turning pro.

Chapter 6

The Sports World's Newest Superstar

Tiger's announcement created a wave of excitement never before seen in the sport of golf. His name was on everyone's lips, even people who did not follow the sport regularly. Butch Harmon, Tiger's coach, felt that Tiger had the tools to compete, but also felt he was going to lose something by turning pro so soon.

"All the amateur titles Tiger has won won't mean anything now," Harmon said. "He'll have to prove himself in a hard environment where there is no mercy. He's got the intelligence and the tools to succeed very quickly. My only worry is that he's losing two of the best years of his life to do something that is very demanding for a young person. Considering everything, though, he's making the right decision. But he's going to have to grow up faster than I'd like him to."

Tiger, however, was growing into more than just pro golf. Because he was deemed such a potentially valuable sports figure, the bidding war for his services was incredible. He was represented by a top management firm, and shortly after he announced he was turning pro, it was revealed that he had signed two huge endorsement deals. One was with the shoe and clothing company, Nike, and the other with Titleist, a company that makes golf balls and clubs. The first figure on the five-year contracts was estimated at a total of $40 million. But soon after, it was thought the contracts would bring Tiger closer to $60 million over five years.

The dollar figures were mind-boggling. Someone pointed out that the Nike deal, worth an estimated $40 million, was even more than the company paid basketball superstar Michael Jordan. So Tiger was already being put up on the same pedestal as the world's most recognizible athlete and commercial spokesman. But he said he didn't want to compete with Jordan or anyone else in pitching products.

"I can enjoy material things, but that doesn't mean I need them," Tiger said. "It doesn't matter to me if I live [in a large, opulent place] or in a shack. I'd be fine in a shack, as long as I could play some golf. I'll do commercials for Nike and for Titleist, but there won't be much more than that. I have no desire to be the king of endorsement money."

Again, it went back to Tiger's upbringing, how his father always taught him to be honest when it came to wants versus needs. He also knew he couldn't afford to get caught up in all the hype, because that would create a drain on his time. His primary business was still playing golf. His management team knew he had to win to remain a hot marketing property. But for Tiger, the desire to win was simply part of his being. When asked how he expected to fare in his first pro tournament, he said, quickly, "I'm playing to win. I have a game plan and it doesn't include finishing second."

Tiger's game plan involved the PGA Tour. Since it was late in the 1996 season, he had to make up some ground quickly. To qualify for the 1997 PGA Tour, he had to win enough money in two months to get himself into the top 125 golfers on the money-winnings list. He would have a chance to do it because a player is allowed seven sponsor's exemptions a year. That meant he could play in seven tournaments before the year was over.

If he didn't make the top 125 and didn't win a tournament, he would have to qualify for the '97 Tour by earning one of the forty some odd spots available at the PGA Tour Qualifying Tournament. That was something he didn't want to do. But he also knew if he won a single tournament, he would be exempt from having to qualify for two years. That meant he could play in as many as he wanted. He hoped the Greater Milwaukee Open would be a starting point.

There were others, of course, who felt Tiger's impact would be much more than simply winning golf tournaments. Because he had a chance to dominate a sport that was almost all white and one not played by that many young people of any race, it was felt that he would have a chance to make a difference, to actually revolutionize golf by bringing many different kinds of young people into the sport. Tim Finchem, the PGA Commissioner, was one of those very excited about Tiger's entrance into the Pro Tour.

"It is conceivable that, in terms of overall impact on the sport," Finchem said, "when you figure the media, the dollars on the table for him, his ability to be a role model—if he succeeds, he might be the most important player ever."

Another who sincerely felt that Tiger was not only a great athlete, but also potentially a very special person, was the family lawyer, John Merchant.

"Other athletes who have risen to this level just didn't have this kind of guidance," Merchant said. "With a father and mother like Tiger's, he *has* to be real. It's such a rare quality in celebrities nowadays. There hasn't been a politician since [former President] John Kennedy whom people have wanted to touch. But watch Tiger. He *has* it. He actually listens to people when they stop him in an airport. He looks them in the eye. I can't ever envision Tiger Woods selling his autograph."

Tiger continued to feel confident that he could handle the media rush he knew would come. He repeated that he wanted to be a role model, that he considered it an honor to have that chance.

"People took time to help me as a kid, and they impacted my life," Tiger explained. "I want to do the same for kids, trying to help out as much as I can. As long as I can touch one person, I feel I've done my job. But I'm definitely going to try to do a whole lot more than that."

Finally, it was time for golf again. The Greater Milwaukee Open is not considered one of golf's bigger tournaments, but with Tiger's entrance the golf course was jammed with spectators and members of the media. ESPN was covering the event for television and the station's motives were made clear when the announcer opened the telecast by saying, "We are here for one reason and one reason only."

That reason was Tiger Woods. When it was finally time, he stepped up to the tee for his first shot as a professional. With every eye on him he took that perfect swing and sent a rocket straight down the fairway, the ball coming to rest some 336 yards from the tee. He would later call it his "most memorable shot of the tournament."

Tiger played fine golf that first day, breaking par with a 67 for eighteen holes. At that point he was in contention to win. He followed it up with a solid 69 the second day, claiming his score would have been lower had he drained a few makeable putts.

"I think I used them up in the Amateur last week," he joked.

But in the third round all the hoopla of the past week caught up with him. He was tired, and it showed. He still managed a 73, but in a tournament that saw many golfers breaking par, a round of 73 took him well out of contention. It was apparent he wouldn't be pulling off any miracles in his debut. He closed the tournament with a solid 68, but still managed to create the most electric moment of the entire weekend.

It happened on the 188-yard, fourteenth hole. Tiger hit his tee shot right at the pin. The ball bounced a couple of times, then rolled onto the green and right into the cup. He had made a hole in one, the ninth of his career! Even though his four-round total of 277 was only good for sixtieth place, he had created the tournament's biggest moment with his ace.

His official winnings for finishing well back were just $2,544.00. Yet Tiger was like a little kid when he got his check. Forget about the millions in endorsements. He looked at the PGA check and said, "That's my money. I *earned* this!"

That wasn't all he earned. Loren Roberts, who won the tournament, chose to talk about Tiger instead of his own victory.

"He's come along at exactly the right time," Roberts said. "He's like Arnold Palmer, a guy who is going to popularize the sport to a bigger audience, to reach out to areas where maybe golf has been slow to reach. He's got a lot on his shoulders. There's no question he's going to do well. When you hit your best shot and look up and he's sixty yards in front of you, that's impressive, to start.

But he's still going to have to beat those other guys out there, and that's not going to be as easy as some people think"

Another veteran pro, Bruce Litzke, who was paired with Tiger during the third round, when he shot his 73, also had nothing but positive things to say.

"I played with him on his bad day, nothing working for him, and yet I was impressed," Litzke said. "You learn about somebody when he's having that kind of day. A lot of twenty-year-olds would get frustrated, angry. He never lost his temper, still kept working. If he's going to be the game's next great ambassador, then the game is in good hands."

As for Tiger, if he was disppointed by his finish, he wasn't complaining. He just seemed genuinely happy to have his debut behind him and to be out on the course again.

"It was just great to get back to what I do, play golf," he said. "That's what I know best. That's what I've always done."

Tiger reiterated his plan to play in the next six tournaments, all his exemption would allow, in order to crack the top 125 in earnings. It would be a tiring schedule, especially for a twenty-year-old who was going to have people pulling him in ten directions at once.

It was, indeed, a whirlwind week following the Greater Milwaukee Open. Tiger's first commercial for Nike began airing nationwide and it caused a

Tiger celebrates with his trademark uppercut after hitting a hole-in-one during the fourth round of the Greater Milwaukee Open, his first professional tournament.

The Tiger Woods Foundation is dedicated to bringing golf to inner-city and minority kids who might otherwise not get the chance to learn the sport. Here Tiger works with a young golfer during a clinic at Buena Vista, Florida, in March of 1997.

Tiger's mother, Kultida, proudly holds an ad announcing Tiger's participation in the Asian Honda Classic, which took place in her home country of Thailand in January of 1997.

The close bond between Tiger and his dad, Earl, was evident as Tiger announced he was turning pro on August 28, 1996.

Tiger receives an appreciative hug from Lee Elder after Tiger became the youngest golfer to win the coveted Masters title in April of 1997. Elder was the first African-American golfer to play the Masters back in 1975.

Jack Nicklaus, one of golf's all-time greats, presents Tiger with the College Player of the Year Award in June of 1996.

Tiger's concentration is evident as he watches an opponent hit during the 1996 NCAA Golf Championship. Tiger won the title representing Stanford University.

After winning the Asian Honda Classic, Tiger receives a Royal Decoration from Thailand's Prime Minister Chaowalit Yong Chaiyudh at the Government House in Bangkok, Thailand.

Tiger was more of a nationwide celebrity than ever after winning the Masters. Just a few days after his record-breaking triumph, Tiger was introduced to a huge ovation during the New York Knicks–Chicago Bulls game in Chicago.

It has always been important to Tiger to *enjoy* golf. Here he jokes during a practice round at the Australian Masters.

Tiger's brilliant approach shot on the 18th hole during the final round of the Masters brought looks of admiration and wonderment from the gallery.

The youngest Masters champion in history shows off the traditional winner's green jacket as well as the championship trophy.

bit of controversy. Over images of Tiger playing golf, he spoke the words, "There are still courses in the United States I am not allowed to play because of the color of my skin. I've heard I'm not ready for you. Are you ready for me?"

Many felt that this was the type of "attitude" piece that had been too prevalent in recent years. They also felt it wasn't what Tiger Woods was all about. The ad ran for a time, but was finally pulled, replaced by softer ads that didn't play on race. Later, Tiger talked about it, looking for the positive side.

"It's not *me* to blow my own horn, the way I come across in that Nike ad," he said, "or to say things quite that way. But I felt it was worth it because the message needed to be said. You can't say something like that in a polite way. Golf has shied away from this for too long."

Tiger knew there would be no way he could ignore the race question altogether. He just had to deal with things as they came and try to make a difference in his own way. To begin with, he said flat out, "I don't consider myself a Great Black Hope." If he was going to be a role model, he hoped it would be for all youngsters.

"I'm just a golfer who happens to be black and Asian," he added. "It doesn't matter whether kids are white, black, brown, or green. All that matters is I touch them the way I can through clinics and whatever else I do, and that they benefit from it."

Tiger, his father, and other advisors were already planning to run golf clinics, and also to organize the Tiger Woods Foundation, which would send sports psychologists into underprivileged neighborhoods to try to instill in children, through golf, a greater sense of self-worth, followed by golf clinics spearheaded by Tiger and his father.

In addition, there were plans for Tiger to become part of the National Minority Golf Foundation, which was headed by his father and a lawyer friend. The Minority Golf Foundation would also try to "help kids in the inner city go to college under golf scholarships, and mostly to help kids in the inner city play golf."

So in some ways, the pressures were building. They were different pressures and commitments from his Stanford and amateur days, but still the kind of things he would have to deal with while trying to play winning golf at the same time. Some people wondered if Tiger could do it, whether the celebrity part of being Tiger Woods would affect the play and tenacity of the golfer who was Tiger Woods. Only time would tell.

Chapter 7

Looking for that First Victory

After his debut tournament and everything surrounding it, Tiger knew he had to concentrate on playing his best golf. While his first pro tournament had produced three sub-70 rounds, as well as that exciting hole in one, the bottom line was that he had finished in sixtieth place. And that was something Tiger didn't like. Sitting that far back in the pack, with fifty-nine golfers shooting a better score, wasn't something he was used to, and he had no plans for it to happen again.

The next tour stop was the Bell Canadian Open. Tiger shot a 70 for each of the first two rounds, then lowered his score to 68 in round three. But the fourth round never took place. Rainy weather caused officials to end the tourney after three and Tiger was officially credited with an eleventh place finish. It was better than his first tourney, but still not vintage Woods. People began to wonder if everyone expected too much, too soon. Maybe the jump from the amateurs to the pros was going to be tougher than anyone thought.

Now it was on to the Quad City Classic in Coal Valley, Illinois, where tournament organizers had to print up additional tickets to meet the demand of fans. The reason for the rush was again Tiger Woods. And this time it began to look as if Tiger might give everyone what they were waiting for—a first place finish. After a 69 in the first round, he caught fire and shot a sensational 64 in round two. When he followed that with a 67, he was up among the leaders and in a good position to win. Known for his strong finishes, it looked as if this might be the week.

But during the fourth round disaster struck, in the form of something that simply wasn't supposed to happen to Tiger. He actually four-putted one hole to take a quadruple-bogey 8, four strokes over par. That hole led to his final round 72, and took away any chance to win. He finished with a 272 and a tie for fifth place. It still wasn't a victory, but he was getting closer. A top-five finish puts you up among the elite.

His fourth tournament was the B.C. Open in Endicott, New York. Once again, Tiger was in a great position to win. He shot 68-66-66 for the first three rounds and was in a tie for third place. Once again, however, repeated bad weather caused the tournament to be called before the final round could be played. So Tiger was credited with a tie for third. But with a tie for fifth and tie for third in his last two tournaments, he seemed to be getting into that good groove.

The next tournament was the Buick Challenge in Pine Mountain, Georgia. That same week he was also scheduled to appear at the Fred Haskins Award Dinner, where he was slated to receive an award as 1996 College Player of the Year. But while preparing for the tournament, Tiger suddenly made a decision that would precipitate the first real crisis of his professional career.

After a long practice round, part of his regular weekly routine, he flopped down on a sofa. A few minutes later he got up and began to walk across the room. He stopped suddenly in his tracks.

"I couldn't even remember what I'd just gotten off the couch for, two seconds before," he related. "I was like mashed potatoes. Total mush."

Tiger felt completely drained, exhausted. The grind of the last month had finally taken its toll. He simply didn't feel he could go through with the tournament and play his best golf. So he withdrew, and the fallout started immediately. Tournament organizers were understandably upset. After all, Tiger was already the number-one draw on the circuit. Many tickets had been sold to people coming for just one reason—to see Tiger play.

In addition, because he was going home to rest, he also said he could not attend the Fred Haskins Award Dinner. The double pullout really brought out the critics, and many of them were his fellow pros.

"I can't ever remember being tired when I was twenty," said Tom Kite. Another pro, Peter Jacobson, added that "You can't compare Tiger to [Jack] Nicklaus and [Arnold] Palmer because they never [walked out]."

Veteran pro Davis Love III also said he felt Tiger had made a big mistake. "Everybody's been telling him how great he is," Love said. "I guess he's started to believe it."

Curtis Strange implied that Tiger was ungrateful for an invitation (to the tournament) that had been given to help him get into the groove of the tour as quickly as possible. Even the legendary Arnold Palmer, who had acted as a friend and mentor since Tiger turned pro, said he thought withdrawing was wrong.

"Tiger should have played," Palmer said. "He should have also gone to the dinner. You don't make commitments you can't fulfill unless you are on your deathbed, and I don't believe he was."

At first, Tiger was really stung by the criticism. "I thought those people were my friends," he said. The harsh reality of the sudden attacks by his fellow pros also made him think about what could have been.

"I miss college," he admitted. "I miss hanging out with my friends, getting in a little trouble, sitting around and talking half the night. There's no one my own age to hang out with anymore, because almost everyone my age is still in college. I have to be so guarded. I'm a target for everybody now and there's nothing I can do about it. My mother was right when she said that turning pro would take away my youth. But, golfwise, there was nothing left for me in college."

After thinking about it some more, Tiger realized that what he had done was wrong, that as a professional and a celebrity, you *do* keep commitments once you make them. He sent letters of apology to all 200 people who had planned to attend the Haskins dinner. The dinner was rescheduled a number of weeks later, and this time Tiger spoke graciously of the award and about the mistake he had made.

"I should have attended the dinner [the first time]," he told the audience. "I admit I was wrong, and I'm sorry for any inconvenience I may have caused. But I have learned from that, and I will never make that mistake again. I'm very honored to be part of this select group (College Player of the Year), and I'll always remember, for both good and bad, this Haskins Award; for what I did and what I learned, for the company I'm now in and I'll always be in."

He was a young man learning, a young man growing. Now he wanted to be a young golfer winning. Feeling rested and rejuvenated, Tiger headed to Nevada and the Las Vegas International, one of the few tournaments that was played for five rounds instead of four.

In the opening round, Tiger shot a modest 70. It was the way he had started most of his pro tournaments. Not a great score, but low enough to keep him in contention. Then, in round two, he began to show the kind of great golf that had propelled him to so many titles as an amateur. He shot a sensational 63 to move back into contention. Then, in the third and fourth rounds he was again very solid with a 68 and 67. Had the tournament ended after four rounds, Tiger would have finished in a five-way tie for seventh, four strokes behind the leader. That's how many golfers were bunched together.

But Las Vegas was a five-round tournament, and as soon as Tiger teed off to begin the final round, it was apparent that he was on his game. As always, he was hitting longer than anyone off the tee. But his short game was on, too. On the eleventh hole, he sunk a thirty-foot putt for a birdie. That was after rescuing his tee shot from a sand trap with a beautiful sand wedge pitch onto the edge of the green.

When Tiger sank his final putt on eighteen, he had a 64 for the day and was tied for first with Davis Love III. To show how hot he was, Tiger had played the final seventy-two holes of the ninety-hole tournament twenty-six strokes below par. Now Tiger and Love had to play a sudden death shoot-out for the championship.

It didn't last long. Sudden death is simply another version of match play. First one to win a hole wins the championship. Tiger was used to the pressure in match play from his U.S. Amateur victories. He won the first hole the two played when Love missed a six-foot putt, and with it his first championship as a professional. Without appearing cocky, Tiger said he wasn't really surprised by his win.

"[My first win] should have come at Quad City," he said, of the tournament where he suffered a quadruple bogey in the final round. "I learned a lot from that."

Others weren't surprised he had won, either. His coach, Butch Harmon, also thought it would happen even sooner.

"I'm surprised it took this long," Harmon said. "I'm one of the few people who really knows how good he is. For him, to be able to just play golf was the key. He didn't have to go to school or do anything else."

The other pros were also impressed. Paul Goydos, who had won a tournament earlier in the year, said, "Tiger has a chance to win every single week he plays. This is the third straight time he's had a chance to win. How many guys do that? And how many guys do that when they're twenty?"

Davis Love, beaten in sudden death, still found time to make some interesting observations about Tiger.

"He's not playing for the money," Love said. "He never thought, 'I have to make another one hundred and some thousand dollars to make the top 125.' He's trying to win. He thinks about winning and nothing else. I like the way he thinks. We were all trying to prolong the inevitable. We knew he was going to win. I just didn't want it to be today. Everybody better watch out. He's going to be a force."

Love was right about one thing. There didn't seem to be any pressure on Tiger to make the top 125 in earnings. His prize at Vegas brought his winnings to $437,194. Having played just five tournaments, he was already in 40th place on the money list.

There was another aspect of his game at Las Vegas that had everyone in the golfing world buzzing. Tiger had averaged 323 yards per drive for the ninety holes of the tournament. That was thirteen yards better than the next longest hitter, John Adams, and an average of thirty-eight yards better than the rest of the field.

At six-foot-two and just 160 pounds, he still looked very thin. Many of the tours' long-hitters over the years were the bigger, almost burly men. What was the secret to Tiger's long drives? Butch Harmon noted that Tiger strives to use no more than an eighty percent effort on most tee shots. That leads to a more repeatable swing and greater accuracy. So he wasn't even trying to hit as hard as he could.

The great Jack Nicklaus had mentioned several times that Tiger had "the most fundamentally sound swing I've ever seen." Other experts pointed out that Tiger was able to store remarkable energy on his backswing by making a massive shoulder turn of nearly 120 degrees, while limiting his hip turn to less than 30 degrees.

It was also noted that Tiger had broad shoulders and powerful thighs. His body, while thin, was tightly wrapped with dense muscle. He also had a thirty-five-inch sleeve length (very long for his size) and a rock-hard twenty-eight-inch waist, all of which allows for the speed with which he rotates his torso and hips on the downswing, the fastest in golf.

While at Stanford, Tiger spent countless hours in the weight room, developing his strength and quickness. Karen Branick, who was the assistant strength coach at Stanford and supervised many of Tiger's workouts, said that "Tiger's lean body type allows him to handle a lot of resistance without getting too bulky or losing flexibility."

Tests showed that Tiger made contact with the dead center of the club face with incredible regularity. His drives were also hit with a minimum of backspin and at what is generally considered the ideal angle, nine degrees. But perhaps all the technical jargon was best summed up by Art Sellinger, a two-time national long-drive champion.

"Tiger is technically perfect, and he's so grooved, so repeatable, that he'd be consistent under any kinds of conditions. I've said for a while that somebody was going to come along with the ability to hit it as long as we do and get it in the fairway, and that guy is going to rewrite the books. Guess what? He's here."

And perhaps that's why one writer, beginning his story about Tiger's win at Las Vegas, wrote this simple, seven-word lead.

"Golf, as we know it, is over."

Chapter 8

The Best Start Ever

Tiger's first victory at Las Vegas once again excited the entire sports world. There was already more focus on golf than there had been in years. The sport was now often the lead story on sportscasts instead of being buried far down the list. And the reason was Tiger. There are pros on the tour who don't win a tournament for years. Even with veterans, victories can be few and very far between.

Yet Tiger had tasted triumph in just his fifth pro tournament. It was also the third straight tourney that had seen him finish in the top five. Of his nineteen pro rounds to date, he had broken 70 on fourteen occasions. That in itself was amazing. And in three of the five rounds in which he *didn't* crack that number, he was right at it, an even 70. His poorest round was a 73, the third round of his first tourney in Milwaukee, when fatigue finally caught up with him.

But he still hadn't shot one of those nothing-goes-right rounds when the score might balloon to 78 or even 81. All pros have days like that. Yet the first-year pro Woods had not. More and more people were beginning to view him as a true golfing phenomenon. It was quickly reaching the point where nothing he did surprised anyone.

His next tournament was the LaCantra Texas Open. He didn't win, but he came close. Continuing to play great golf, his 69-68-73-67—277 was good for third place, just two strokes behind the winner—his fourth straight top-five finish. Now it was on to Florida and the Walt Disney/Oldsmobile Classic in Orlando, where Tiger Woods mania was again running rampant.

When Tiger visited Walt Disney World before the tournament began, people followed him everywhere. There was also another famous Orlando resident who was expecting to play a round of golf with Tiger. He couldn't wait for Tiger to get there. And this was a guy who was also used to the adulation of large crowds—baseball superstar Ken Griffey, Jr.

At the Magnolia Golf Course alongside Walt Disney World, it began to look like business as usual. Tiger shot a 69 in the opening round. It always seemed as if his first round never set the world on fire, but always kept him close. There were still a number of golfers ahead of him. At breakfast with his father that morning Tiger was reading about the tournament in the local paper. Suddenly, he put down the paper and looked directly at Earl Woods.

"Pop," he said. "Got to shoot sixty-three today. That's what it will take to get into it."

Not paying that much attention, his father simply said, "So go do it."

Earl Woods wasn't feeling well that day, so instead of walking the golf course, he waited patiently in his motel room, a room that didn't have the channel on its cable system that was telecasting the tournament. Finally, when Tiger returned, the first thing his father asked was his score for the day.

"Sixty-three," Tiger said, as if it was the most natural thing in the world.

"Oh, my god," was his father's answer.

True to his word, Tiger had played brilliantly, firing a 63, which put him up among the leaders and in a great position to win. He followed it with another 69 and moved into the final round looking for his second victory in seven pro tournaments, something very few thought possible. He was paired with veteran Payne Stewart, a former U.S. Open champion. Both golfers had identical 201 scores after three rounds. They would battle head to head for the lead the entire afternoon.

On the front nine the lead seesawed back and forth. Stewart sunk birdie putts on the second and fourth holes to go in front. But Tiger, with his usual propensity for the spectacular, eagled the fourth and birdied the fifth to regain the lead. They duplicated birdies at the seventh and eighth. Then Tiger three-putted the ninth for a bogey, and with nine holes remaining the two golfers were tied again, both at 19 under for the tournament. But the best was yet to come.

Spectators had an added bit of Florida's home-state flavor as Tiger and Stewart were on the sixth green, ready to putt. With the gallery moving and shifting all over for position, a deer suddenly ran out from hiding and across the seventh fairway. Then from a nearby pond, an alligator appeared, making a quick but fruitless run at the deer before scurrying back into the pond. After a brief pause to make sure the area was safe, the tournament resumed.

Tiger started the final nine with a birdie at ten to regain the lead by a stroke. But then he faltered at the next hole, bogeying the eleventh and losing the lead when Stewart nailed another nifty birdie putt. But at the twelfth, the scenario was reversed. Tiger made a beautiful approach shot that put the ball just a foot from the hole. His birdie gave him the lead once more.

It remained close right until the final hole. Tiger still had a one-shot lead. Stewart hit one of his best drives of the tournament, coming within ten yards of Tiger's blast down the fairway. Stewart's approach shot then rolled within eight feet of the hole, while Tiger's stopped thirty feet short. But

Stewart's birdie putt, which could have tied the match, broke left at the last second and left him with a tip-in. Tiger two-putted from thirty feet out to come in with a round of 66, a total of 267, and a victory over Stewart by a single stroke.

The one thing that sullied the victory ever so slightly was that a rookie pro named Taylor Smith, playing behind Woods and Stewart, finished strong to tie Tiger at 267. But shortly after finishing, Taylor learned he had been disqualified for using a putter with grips that did not conform to the USGA specifications. The disqualification kept Tiger from having to face Taylor in a sudden death playoff.

"This is very gratifying," Tiger said afterward. "But I do have some mixed emotions. I feel like I should have been in a play-off with Taylor. It's unfortunate, what happened to him, because he played his heart out."

Again, Tiger was being a true sportsman, but the other golfers, including Taylor, said tournament officials had done the right thing. He had unwittingly broken the rules. The victory belonged to Tiger Woods.

During the postmatch interviews, someone asked Tiger why he had done so well in the pros when his best finish in a pro tournament as an amateur was just twenty-second. Again he had a logical answer.

"When I played in those tournaments [as an amateur], I was either in high school or college," he explained. "I'd get dumped into the toughest places to play, and usually was trying to study, get papers done, and everything else. I knew if I came out there and played every single day, I'd get into a rhythm, and I have."

His fellow pros were beginning to realize more and more that Tiger was the real thing as a golfer and as a person, someone who was going to help the entire sport.

"All the accolades need to go to Tiger for the way he's played and conducted himself over the last eight weeks," said Payne Stewart. "He's a wonderful player and the shot in the arm our tour needed."

John Cook mentioned how Tiger's attitude was markedly different from that of many of the pros on tour.

"There are a lot of guys out here who come into a tournament thinking, well, 8 under will get me top-25," Cook said. "They figure that will be all right. Now here comes this kid [Tiger] who's ripping and shaking from the first tee."

What Cook was saying was that many players simply pointed to a top-25 or top-10 finish, figuring that gave them a nice paycheck for the tournament and would allow them to finish in the top 125 and keep their exemption. Tiger was coming out week after week with just one objective. To win the tournament.

The great Jack Nicklaus, already a big Tiger fan, saw his start on the tour as heralding a new era.

"I don't think we've had a whole lot happen [on the tour] in what, ten years?" Nicklaus said. "I mean, some guys have come on and won a few tournaments, but nobody has sustained and dominated. I think we might have somebody now."

With so many fine golfers in each tournament, it's very difficult for one or two golfers to dominate. A pro who wins two or three tournaments in a single year has had a great year. Tiger had now won two of his first seven and was on a run of five straight top-5 finishes. For a seasoned pro that would be outstanding. For a rookie, it was next to incredible.

That wasn't all. For winning yet another tournament, Tiger received $216,000 in prize money. That brought his winnings for the year to $734,794, nearly three-quarters of a million dollars. His goal had been to finish in the top 125. Now he was twenty-third on the money list and he had only been playing for two months. Another win and he would be over the one million dollar mark. It was just remarkable.

So were the galleries. For the first time ever at PGA events there were many youngsters, teenagers watching and nearly all rooting for Tiger. There were also faces of many minority youngsters—African-Americans, Hispanics, Asians—who had never attended golf tournaments before. Many of them yelled for Tiger, cheered and rooted for him, tried to high-five him as he walked the course.

Despite his intensity, Tiger often returned the

high-fives, said thank you to fans who cheered for him and encouraged him, and also threw extra golf balls to kids during the round.

"I remember when I was a kid," he said. "I always wanted to be part of it [a golf tournament]. I always wanted to be connected somehow."

By acknowledging his fans, signing autographs, giving away golf balls, and simply high-fiving them, he was allowing them to be connected. And hopefully, many of them who knew little about the sport before Tiger would now look for ways to try learning and playing golf on their own.

But that still wasn't all. There was also the numbers, the stats, the comparisons. A compilation of Tiger's first seven tournaments showed conclusively that he had rocked the pro tour in a way no golfer had before him. It was already an undisputable fact.

In his seven pro tournaments Tiger had a scoring average of 67.89 strokes per round. He didn't play enough to qualify for year-end honors, but that was not only the best of the year, but below the record of 68.81 set by Greg Norman in 1994. And had he played enough to qualify he would have been the 1996 leader in three other categories. His average of 302.8 yards per drive was fourteen yards better than the official leader, John Daly. His 4.68 birdies per round and ratio of one eagle for every 55 holes was also tops on the tour.

With all that, Tiger sounded even more of a warning when he said, "It may be surprising to some guys, but it's not surprising to people who know me, but I haven't really played my best yet. I've hit the ball pretty good, but not the greatest. And I haven't had the greatest putting round yet."

Hearing that, veteran pro Peter Jacobson, who hadn't had one top-5 finish all year said, "If this is how he is every week, then it's over. Then he's the greatest player in the history of the game."

And what about the great players who came before? The two men credited with rejuvenating the modern game—Arnold Palmer and Jack Nicklaus—just didn't come close to the kind of start that Tiger had. Neither won a tournament in their first seven starts, but the difference was even more startling.

In seven tournaments, Tiger's finishes were T60, 11, T5, T3, 1, 3, 1. The "T" stands for finishing in a tie. Palmer, in his first seven, finished T10, T44, T6, T22, T41, T18, and T21. Nicklaus's finishes were T50, T15, T23, T47, T32, T2, T17. It certainly wasn't a matter of the tour being tougher in the 1950s and 1960s. It's simply more a matter of Tiger just coming in and dominating without needing any period of adjustment.

Round by round is also interesting. In the twenty-seven rounds Tiger played in those seven tournaments, he shot under 70 an amazing twenty-one times. Palmer managed to do it twelve times in twenty-eight rounds, while Nicklaus struggled to break 70 just five times in twenty-nine rounds. By strokes, Tiger averaged 67.89 per round. Palmer was at 70.40, while Nicklaus came in at 71.89, a full four strokes more per round than Tiger.

It didn't take long for the perception of Tiger to change a full 180 degrees. Instead of wondering how Tiger was going to fare against the best golfers in the world, people were now wondering how the best golfers in the world could possibly beat him.

Chapter 9

Traveling the World

The final tournament of the year was the Tour Championship at Tulsa, Oklahoma. Only a small number of pros qualify to play. Whether Tiger would have won is a matter of conjecture. All chances to finish first, or even in the top five disappeared at 2 A.M., just hours before the start of the second round. That's when Tiger received a phone call from his mother, informing him that his father had just suffered a second heart attack. They were rushing him to a hospital right there in Tulsa.

Earl Woods's first heart attack came when Tiger was just ten. That one hadn't slowed him down much. But this one had everyone concerned. Tiger spent the rest of the night at the hospital. Only when it was determined that his father was in no immediate danger did he return to the golf course to play the second round.

"There are things more important than golf," he said, succinctly.

So Tiger played the second round with virtually no sleep and shot the poorest round of his pro career, a 78. It all but took him out of contention. Checking on his father's condition every chance he had, Tiger nevertheless finished the tourney in a tie for twenty-first place. The check he received brought his earnings for the year to $790,594, good for twenty-fourth place. Not bad for a rookie with just eight tournaments under his belt.

Thus it came as no surprise when he was named PGA Tour Rookie of the Year once the season ended. Shortly after, he received an even higher honor. *Sports Illustrated* magazine named Tiger their 1996 Sportsman of the Year. In choosing him for the prestigious prize, the magazine called him "the rare athlete to establish himself *immediately* as the dominant figure in his sport."

In December, Tiger was set to play in the Skins Game, a made-for-television event where a few select golfers play for large sums of money on each hole. Before the event began, it was revealed that Tiger had received a number of death threats through the mail. Once that came out, Tiger's management team admitted that he had been receiving hate mail ever since he turned pro. Interestingly enough, the first instinct at the agency was to just trash the hate and racist mail that arrived. But Tiger insisted on seeing every single piece of it. He even admitted that he had kept one particularly cruel letter taped to his wall when he was at Stanford.

"People often tend to lose sight of who they are," Tiger said. "By looking at all the mail that comes in, I'm reminded of who I am, and I think that's important."

As his father had taught him years earlier, Tiger wasn't becoming bitter. Rather he was turning his anger into a positive. It motivated him to do even better. So when he arrived at the Mercedes Championships at La Costa Resort and Spa in Carlsbad, California, the first tournament of 1997, he had the same burning desire to win.

Tiger came to California after four weeks of rest and relaxation with his friends. He traveled to Las Vegas to celebrate his twenty-first birthday and usher in the New Year. So it wasn't surprising when he showed some rust in the opening round. But he still managed a credible 70, his usual start, putting him in a position to make all those in front of him wary.

He stayed near the top after the second round, then began chasing down Tom Lehman, who was the defending British Open champ, the 1996 leading money winner and Player of the Year. So, once again, Tiger was after one of the best. He closed the third round with four straight birdies to tie Lehman at 14-under for the tournament with one round left. One of his birdies was on the 569-yard, seventeenth hole. After a huge drive off the tee, he became just the second player in tournament history to reach the green in two shots. His long hitting amazed everyone all over again.

Tiger was now looking forward to the final round. But it never came. Instead it rained and the course became all but unplayable. Tournament officials decided the only way to settle the championship was to have Tiger and Lehman play a sudden death shoot-out. They chose a short hole, the 188-yard, par-3 seventh, for the simple reason it was the only hole deemed playable in the heavy rain.

Lehman was set to hit first. He took a six iron, gauged his shot, then swung. The swing didn't look smooth, and Lehman's body language immediately after impact showed he had mis-hit the ball. It hooked to the left. The wind caught it and it fell smack into a small pond on the left side of the green. He had to take a penalty stroke. All Tiger had to do was put the ball on the green and the tournament was his.

He took off his black jacket to reveal a bright red shirt underneath. Red was always the color he wore in the final round of a tournament when he felt he could win. Tiger also used a six iron. Only his shot went straight at the pin. It landed two feet to the right of the hole, then spun back to within six inches of the cup. The gallery erupted at the great shot Tiger had made under trying conditions.

"When the elements are against you," Tiger said, "it's easier to hit a bad shot. So I had the advantage of hitting second. When it was my turn, all I thought about was where I wanted my ball to go, which was to the right of the pin. That's where it ended up, right?''

But within six inches? Needless to say, Tiger holed out and had his third tournament victory in nine starts. He had won three PGA tournaments faster than any other player in history. Sam Snead was the only one who came close, winning his first three in eleven tries back in 1936 and 1937. The victory also gave Tiger more than $1 million in career earnings. That was also a record. Before Tiger, Ernie Els held the record, winning his first million in twenty-eight tournaments. Tiger did it in nine.

"Tiger is stunning all of us," said Els, when informed that his record had been broken.

Runner-up Lehman tried to put up a brave front, stating that the other pros weren't about to just hand the tournaments to Tiger.

"Guys out here are competitive," Lehman said. "They're not going to lie down for somebody. Tiger's going to be a great player. There's no doubt in my mind he's going to be one of the best ever, but he has to earn it."

Yet a short time later, Lehman talked about the task it would have been going against Tiger in the final eighteen holes of a close tournament. He didn't sound optimistic.

"If I go out and play well and lose, I'm going to know there's a new kid on the block who's just way better than everybody else," Lehman explained. "Tom Lehman is the player of the year, but Tiger

Woods is probably the player of the next two decades. I'm not sure if I feel like the underdog or what, but it's a unique situation. It's almost like trying to hold off the inevitable, like bailing water out of a sinking boat."

The expectations were increasing. People were beginning to get used to Tiger winning, and before long anything other than a victory would be disappointing, especially to the throngs coming out to watch Tiger win. But being realistic and often sounding wise beyond his years, Tiger knew he might have to deal with expectations that would not be easy to satisfy.

"I've been thinking about this [the expectations] more and more," he said. "People can say all kinds of things about me and Nicklaus, and make me into whatever. But it still comes down to one thing. I've still got to hit the shot. Me. Alone. That's what I must never forget."

Looking ahead, Tiger also knew that people would be judging his ultimate success by how he did in the four major tournaments—the Masters, U.S. Open, British Open, and PGA Tournaments. The Masters was the first, in mid-April. Those who knew him best said that was the tournament Tiger wanted to win most of all. But before he would travel to Augusta, Georgia, for that one, he had several tournaments to play, including a few that would take him out of the country.

In early February, Tiger was in Pebble Beach, California, for the Pebble Beach National Pro-Am.

The favorite was veteran Mark O'Meara, based on his having won that tournament four previous times. But by now, many people were wondering how anyone could bet against Tiger Woods. In the mind's eye of some, Tiger was the favorite as soon as he picked up a club.

If it came down to Tiger and O'Meara vying for the title, there would be even more interest. Tiger had recently moved to Orlando, Florida, and lived in the same secluded housing complex as O'Meara. The twenty-one-year-old phenom and forty-year-old veteran had become fast friends, golfing together for fun, and fishing together in their spare time. Yet O'Meara said he would relish the challenge of playing his young friend.

"I've been [playing professionally] for seventeen years," O'Meara said. "If I can't handle the pressure, I should get another job."

For two rounds it didn't look as if O'Meara or anyone else would have to worry about Tiger. He played the first two rounds in a combined 142, a sluggish score that left him a full ten strokes behind the leader, David Duval. However, with Tiger Woods, no lead is a big lead. Tiger had the ability to make up strokes with a suddenness that bordered on the impossible.

He began to make his move with a 63 in the third round. He still trailed Duval by 7 and O'Meara by 4. But when the final round came on that Sunday, the crowds were out again, all cheering for another patented Tiger Woods finish. Soon it began looking as if they might get it. Tiger ripped through the front nine in just thirty-one strokes, bringing him within two shots of both Duval and O'Meara.

And as the back nine got under way, Duval faded somewhat. Now the focus was on the two friends, Woods and O'Meara. Tiger was still two strokes back when he birdied the twelfth hole to pull within one. But on the next hole, number thirteen, he missed a putt and had to settle for a bogey, dropping him two back once more. It would be a hole he would remember later.

Tiger parred both the fourteenth and fifteenth, and it seemed as if he might have run out of miracles. But then he birdied both sixteen and seventeen, making his putts and reacting with his trademark uppercut with his clenched fist. Yet O'Meara refused to fold. O'Meara matched Tiger with a birdie of his own on sixteen and then holed a ten-foot putt for a birdie on seventeen.

"When we play together for fun," O'Meara had said earlier, "I tell him, 'Don't give me that pumped-fist deal. I'm going to bury you.'"

True to his word, O'Meara stood up to the pressure and took a one-stroke lead into the final hole. Tiger knew he had to try for an eagle on the par-5 eighteenth. After a big tee shot, his second shot carried 267 yards and onto the green. But the ball was still forty feet from the cup. O'Meara chose to play it safe. His second shot was short of the green and in the rough. Tiger had a chance.

O'Meara's third shot, though, was a beauty, a soft chip that rolled to within a foot of the cup.

Tiger then missed his forty-footer for an eagle. Both made their birdie putts and O'Meara had a one-stroke victory over Tiger, and also David Duval, who came back to tie for second. Yet it was Tiger's 63-64 on the final two rounds that created much of the excitement for the tourney.

"You cannot put a dollar sign around pride," said O'Meara, afterward. "I've got a lot of pride. That's what drives me. I was pretty jacked [going up against Tiger]. He's the hottest player in golf right now."

Though Tiger is never happy when he doesn't win, at least he could share a bit in his friend's victory.

"I'm feeling both disappointment and elation," Tiger said. "I should have been in a play-off if not for that bogey."

That was the bogey back on thirteen. Like a baseball pitcher who always remembers what kind of pitch he threw in a tight situation, Tiger remembered each hole and how it fit into the entire match. And while he couldn't win them all, he showed once again that he could never be counted out of a tournament, no matter how far behind he was at any given point.

There was more on Tiger's mind than golf when he left for Thailand, his mother's home country, in early February. Earl Woods had never recovered completely from his second heart attack the previous October. He remained behind to prepare for heart bypass surgery, the operation scheduled after Tiger and his mother returned.

But the commitment had been made earlier. Tiger would be made an honorary citizen of Thailand and would participate in the Asian Honda Classic. After a tiring, twenty-hour plane flight, Tiger was treated like a hero in his mother's country. Both he and Tida were honored at several state ceremonies. Then, when Tiger went out to play in the pro-am competition the day before the official tournament, he was suddenly overcome by the ninety-five-degree heat and humid air. It was a combination of heat exhaustion and a slight case of food poisoning.

Not wanting to disappoint all the people who came to see him in action on the golf course, Tiger returned the next day to play in the tournament. His strength coming back, he started to hit the ball like the Tiger Woods everyone had read about. Not surprisingly, he won the tournament by a comfortable ten shots. Up to his usual tricks in the final round, he had five birdies and nearly eagled the fourth hole. He had a 4-under-par 68 in round four to finish with a 20-under-par 268 for the event.

As he strode down the final fairway, the huge gallery chanted "Ti-GUH, Ti-GUH, Ti-GUH," as they applauded. For his efforts, Tiger received a $48,000 first prize, which paled in comparison to his $480,000 appearance fee. At age twenty-one, he was already becoming a worldwide celebrity.

That night, Tiger was presented with the royal decoration of Thailand by the prime minister. When he accepted the honor, Tiger called his mother to his side, then credited his parents for the man he had become and also for his achievements on the golf course. He told his audience why his father couldn't be there. Then he said, "Papa, I love you. Tonight is special. It shows what happens when two loving people really care and share with a child. Without their teaching, without their love, quite honestly, I wouldn't be here."

Once again Tiger showed that he had not forgotten his own roots and what had gotten him to the top. Sure, much of it came from his own innate character, his love of the game, and his desire to be the best. But the foundation set down by his parents gave him the values and standards by which to live. It was truly a family effort.

For Tiger, there was no time to rest and enjoy the country. That night, he had to leave and catch a flight to Melbourne, Australia, where he would be competing in the Australian Masters the following Thursday. Still worried about his father, and tired from the whirlwind succession of plane flights, golf tournaments, and celebrations, Tiger was not at the top of his game in the tourney.

Uncharacteristically, he started with a 68, then went up to a 70, then a 72. By then he pretty much knew he wouldn't win.

"I'm hitting good putts, but they seem to not want to go in," he said. "I'm all around the edges."

That was the mark of a tired golfer. This time Tiger didn't charge in the final round to win. Now he just wanted to get home and be with his father. When it came to his family, golf always took second place.

TIGER WOODS: A Biography

Earl Woods had triple bypass surgery in late February at the UCLA Medical Center. The operation went well, and Mr. Woods convinced Tiger to play in the Nissan Open at the Riviera Country Club in Pacific Palisades, California. Since the tournament wasn't far from the hospital in Los Angeles where his father was staying, Tiger agreed to play. But again, the worry about his father's health seemed to affect his golf.

"My dad's doing better," Tiger told the press. "He's on the road to recovery, which is perfect, ideal." Then he added, "It's tough for me to play when I know my dad's in the hospital."

His words proved prophetic. He simply didn't have a good tournament. In fact, by the end of the third round he was seven shots back of the leader, England's Nick Faldo. Trailing in the final round normally didn't faze Tiger, not the way he could make up strokes. But this time he just didn't sound like the Tiger who seemed to perform miracles at the end of 1996.

"I just couldn't find it today," he said. "I couldn't drive well. I'm having a difficult time. I know what's happening, but it's still difficult."

Then Tiger basically admitted what was happening. "I'm not going to practice now," he said, rejecting his usual post-round routine. "I'm going to go home and see my pop."

Earl Woods was recovering nicely, and close to being released from the hospital. Tiger decided he was going to stay home until he was sure his father was well. He quickly informed organizers of the next tournament, the Doral-Ryder Open in Miami, Florida, that he was withdrawing, and that he would remain with his father in Los Angeles.

So he didn't win the Nissan and didn't go to the Doral-Ryder, but he was where he wanted to be. That was at his father's side. At the same time, the millions of Tiger Woods fans were beginning to wonder if their hero had suddenly lost the magic.

Chapter 10

The Masters—Part One

The Masters was the first of golf's yearly quartet of major tournaments, and was always played at the Augusta National Golf Course in Augusta, Georgia. It was a club that not a single African-American was allowed to join until 1991. Lee Elder, the fine African-American golfer, became the first black man to play at the Masters in 1975. Though Augusta National was a beautiful course in a beautiful setting, it wasn't a place where men of color were always welcome.

One of the founders of the tournament was once quoted as saying, "As long as I'm alive, golfers will be white, and caddies will be black." Such a statement does not belong in the world of the 1990s, but Augusta National remained a place where a minority golfer might not feel entirely comfortable.

The tournament was the youngest of the four "majors," beginning in 1934. A golfer named Horton Smith won the first ever Masters, but the two most prolific winners of this prestigious tournament were the two golfers who helped the sport grow and expand in the 1950s, 1960s, and 1970s. Arnold Palmer won the tournament four times between 1958 and 1964, while Jack Nicklaus held the Masters' record with six titles. Nicklaus won for the first time in 1963 and for the sixth and final time in 1986, nearly a quarter of a century later.

England's Nick Faldo was the defending champion. In fact, Faldo won for the third time in 1996 and another victory would tie him with Palmer. He was the early favorite. But as had been the case since the previous August, the player most people wanted to see was Tiger Woods.

With his rugged travel schedule and concern over his father's health, it hadn't been a super year so far. Tiger hadn't won a PGA event since the Mercedes in January (the Asian Honda Classic was not a PGA-sanctioned event). And, remember, people were always expecting him to win. In addition, his recent erratic performance was also reason for concern. But now Earl Woods was well on the road to recovery and would be at Augusta to watch his son perform. Still, the Masters was one tournament where Tiger might not get by on raw skills alone.

A major tournament in golf was like a major tournament in tennis (Wimbledon, the U.S. Open), the World Series in baseball, Super Bowl in football, NBA finals in basketball. There was simply more pressure. And, as a rule of thumb, the more experienced players and teams seemed to prevail. Sometimes a team or player had to simply be there one time, get used to the pressure and the atmosphere, then come back the next time and win.

That seemed to be the prevailing feeling about Tiger in the weeks preceeding the Masters, when the hype and excitement began to build. The consensus was that Tiger had the tools to win, but not the experience.

As an amateur, Tiger had played in the Masters twice. In 1995, he was the only amateur to make the cut, though he failed to finish in the top twenty-five. Then in 1996, the year he won the U.S. Amateur and later turned pro, he failed to make the cut. Experts pointed out that he had the same problem both years. His iron shots were long and he often left himself with dangerous downhill putts and difficult chips off the green.

"I've made a lot of mistakes playing Augusta," Tiger admitted, "basically positioning my ball on the green and certain places where I have to miss a shot. It wasn't my game plan to attack the course aggressively."

Tiger also said he had some flaws in his swing at Masters time a year earlier. This is not an uncommon thing with any golf pro. It's almost like a baseball player in a batting slump. Suddenly your swing isn't what you want it to be, and it can often be a difficult thing to correct.

"The problem was at the top of my swing. It caused me to hit a couple of balls long," he said.

Tiger also talked about the tricky fairways at Augusta.

"You stand on the tee and the fairway looks fifty yards wide," he said. "It takes a while to realize there is only ten yards of that fairway you want to be on."

What Tiger meant was the placement of the drives from the tee was very important. There is only about a ten-yard-wide area that gives the golfer a clean shot at the green. Stray outside the ten-yard area, and the ball might still be in the fairway but the approach to the green becomes much more difficult.

Three-time winner Nick Faldo said he felt experience was the key to winning.

"There is a route around Augusta and you have to follow it," Faldo said, adding that he had to play in six or seven Masters before he fully understood the path around the course. That path, incidentally, varies with each of the four rounds because the pin positions on the greens are changed. The hole or cup might be at the upper right side of the green one day, and the lower left the next. That means a golfer's approach shot might be entirely different from day to day.

Veteran Nick Price, another favorite, felt that putting could be the key to winning.

"Augusta is a putting contest," Price said. "If you don't have a 9-1/2 putting game going into Augusta, you are playing for place."

In other words, Price was saying that a golfer must come in to Augusta putting at the top of his game. He's got to sink all the easy putts, and make some of the tougher ones. Otherwise, he doesn't have a chance to win.

Mark O'Meara, Tiger's close friend who had beaten him at Pebble Beach earlier in the year, felt that the focus on Tiger with the press and media was an advantage for the other golfers.

"The attention Tiger gets takes a lot of pressure off the other guys," O'Meara said. "Phil Mickelson and Paul Stankowski are great young golfers [both capable of winning]."

When Masters week arrived, there was even more attention being focused on Tiger. It seemed as if he was the entire story while the rest of the golfers were just secondary. And when he began to shoot his practice rounds early in the week (the tournament, like most, ran from Thursday through Sunday), he was the focus of attention everywhere he went. He was bombarded by requests to attend charity events and make other appearances in the area. With a major tournament approaching, it was all too much.

"People just want to get a piece of your time," he said. "Unfortunately, there are only twenty-four hours in the day and I can't please everybody. Sometimes you have to learn how to say no. That's one thing I have to learn."

As for the Masters, Tiger's confidence appeared to be growing as the tournament approached.

"I think I have the game that if things go my way,

I might have a chance to win this tournament," he said, after playing his final nine holes of practice. "I came here to win and do my best. I just want to stay as patient as possible. I'm hitting crisp shots with my irons and tee shots, and I'm swinging a lot better. I'm also putting real well. I'm rolling the ball better than I have in a long time. Plus, I'm tournament-tough. I don't have to write papers and prepare for finals like I did last year when I was still at Stanford. I've prepared myself mentally and physically for this [tournament]."

Some of the the top pros still seemed skeptical about Tiger's chances. Maybe they just didn't want to admit to themselves that they had to contend with an emerging superstar who would dominate their sport.

"Tiger will probably be a favorite everywhere he goes now," said Greg Norman, the Australian golfer who had blown a six-stroke lead in the final round the year before. "He's won early. He's got the charisma people look at and want to write about. But like I was in my younger days, length is not everything. It's controlling the ball. The distance you hit the ball with your iron shots is the most important factor around here."

Norman was saying that Tiger wouldn't win automatically just because he could hit the ball farther than anyone else. Defending champ Faldo, who was set to be paired with Tiger as the glamour duo in the opening round, said that Tiger would be under more pressure than the others.

"I think there's a learning curve to playing

Augusta," said Faldo, "when to hit the ball, when to make the par and walk. [Tiger] has got an awful lot of pressure and an awful lot of attention on him. But as he said, he's used to it."

And while people were reluctant to talk about it, there was the added burden of race. Everyone knew that no African-American or golfer of mixed race had ever won at Augusta. And there would always be a faction who didn't want to see a man of color win. As one reporter heard an unidentified fan say, "I don't want to see a lot of the homeboy attitude of the basketball court come into the golf world."

It was the kind of subtle racial remark and attitude that Tiger would always encounter, no matter how much he won. Since basketball has become a predominantly African-American sport, and a sport sometimes filled with too much of an in-your-face and showboating attitude, the implication was clear.

But another spectator, who happened to be white, took the other approach. He was a golf fan, and acknowledged how much Tiger had already done for the sport.

"A lot of people who weren't interested in golf know who Tiger Woods is," the man said, as he watched Tiger practice prior to the tournament. "If he's in the hunt on Sunday, twice as many people will be watching than usual. I think the whole country is pulling for him."

To show how far the admiration for Tiger had

gone, there was a quote from Michael Jordan, the world's greatest basketball player and avid golfer, that Tiger had become Michael's only living hero. As of late February, Tiger acknowledged that the two had talked by phone several times, but had not yet met. At that time, when he heard about Michael's naming him his hero, Tiger said, "Yeah, I think it's kind of cool that he says something so polite. Mike is obviously a heck of a ballplayer, but he's a good guy, too. [Golf] is a sport he likes. Who knows, you might see him [on the Senior Tour] when he's fifty."

Since that time, the two had talked more. Tiger was said to have called Michael for advice, specifically on handling the adulation of a hero-worshipping public. Once they met, they became fast friends. Tiger's fame and popularity were reaching out everywhere.

As tee-off time approached on Thursday, April 10, there was little doubt that Tiger Woods was the big story. Tiger's father was also there to cheer his son on. Mr. Woods wasn't well enough yet to walk the entire course, but he would be out there with his wife, watching his son play the biggest tournament of his life. Earl Woods had once predicted that his son would win fourteen majors before he was through. The great Jack Nicklaus had said Tiger would win ten Masters during his career. Brash predictions to make before a golfer had played a single major as a pro. More pressure? Maybe. But remember all those lessons in mental toughness father had given son. Now was the real time to see how Tiger would respond. Par for the Augusta National Course was 72. In the six rounds Tiger had played at Augusta as an amateur in 1995 and 1996, he had never once broken par. But now he was playing for keeps, as a pro.

There was a huge gallery present as Tiger and defending champion Nick Faldo finally teed off. This was supposed to be the day's most exciting pairing, between the three-time champ and the young heir to the throne. Many thought that one of the two would eventually don the traditional green jacket given the winner on Sunday afternoon. But the way things began, both golfers looked like a couple of amateurs struggling to compete with the big guys.

Tiger began the first hole with an errant drive and wound up with a bogey. The same thing happened on the fourth and then the eighth. Those watching him noticed a kind of flinch in his swing off the tees. He was already over par and falling behind those golfers who had started quickly. Faldo wasn't playing much better. His whole game seemed in disarray.

When Tiger bogeyed the ninth hole after another less-than-perfect tee shot, he had finished the front nine four strokes over par at 40. If he continued on this track he might play himself out of contention after just one round. Even the crowds were strangely quiet. There were more disappointing *ooooohs* and *aaaahs* for bad shots than outright cheers.

In addition, the statisticians went running to the record books and quickly announced that no golfer had ever won the Masters after shooting the front nine of the first round in 40. The highest previous first-round front nine that eventually produced a winner was a 38. Was Tiger done already?

At this point, a lesser player might have panicked and begun trying too hard to make up strokes. To approach the game like that could mean a real disaster, a score of 80 or above. If that happened to Tiger he would have to struggle just to make the cut and have virtually no chance to win. Not a single person or fellow golfer at the Augusta National, or, for that matter, any one of the millions watching on television, could have known then what was about to happen. And it would begin at the ten hole, the start of the back nine.

Tiger did something that few athletes have ever done. Usually, if there is a problem with a swing, whether it be with a golf club or baseball bat, it takes time to correct it. A coach or teammate will see it and point it out, or the athlete will view some videotape and realize what he's doing wrong. Even then, it sometimes takes a while to correct the bad habit and get the swing back where it should be. But Tiger actually realized his flaw and corrected it in his mind. Then he was able to make the adjustment immediately, and the results showed.

"I was bringing the club almost parallel to the ground on my backswing," he said, later. "That was way too long for me. I knew I had to shorten the swing."

So Tiger stepped up to the tee on the 485-yard, par-4 tenth hole and blasted a long drive right down the middle of the fairway. Then he hit a beautiful two iron from the fairway to the green and birdied the hole with a nifty eighteen-foot putt. There were murmurs from the gallery as the word spread quickly that Tiger was starting to come around.

On the twelfth hole, he hit a beautiful chip-shot from behind the green that rolled in for another birdie. At the par-5 thirteenth hole he reached the green in two, then two-putted for another birdie. At the 500-yard, par-5 fifteenth hole, Tiger sent a mammoth drive down the center of the fairway. Then he used a wedge to put the ball within four feet of the hole. Most golfers don't have the power to use a wedge for a long second shot. When he holed the putt he had a two-under-par eagle, and the crowd went wild. This was the Tiger Woods they had come to see.

He finished with a birdie-par on seventeen and eighteen. To the amazement of nearly everyone, he had ripped through the back nine in a six-under-par 30, giving him a 2-under-par score of 70 for the round. Nick Faldo, on the other hand, hadn't been able to solve his problems and finished the round with a 75.

Tiger had come from a disastrous start to find himself in fourth place. The relatively unknown John Huston had the first-round lead with a 67. Paul Stankowski was at 68, and Paul Azinger at 69. Then came Tiger, now in a perfect position to make a real run. Some of the other big names did not fare as well. Mark O'Meara shot a 75, Tom Lehman had a 73, Phil Mickelson came in at 76, while Greg Norman shot a 77.

"I was pretty ticked off at the way I played the front nine," Tiger said afterward. "But I dug down deep, and I think that's a sign of maturity in my game."

No one knew it then, but the best was yet to come.

Chapter II

The Masters—Part Two

While every round of a golf tournament is important, it has been said that the last two rounds of the Masters are what separates the men from the boys. But the better position a golfer is in at the beginning of those rounds, the better chance he has. So second-round play—the one that generates the least excitement—is when those making the cut jockey for the best position.

As soon as the second round began it was apparent that Tiger was not going to repeat his first day's play on the front nine. Rather, it looked as if he was taking right up from where he left off after the back nine. He birdied the second hole and after taking his only bogey of the day on three, birdied five and eight. Then on the ninth hole he did something that had the entire gallery buzzing with disbelief.

Tiger's drive hooked into a clump of tall pine trees, leaving him what seemed like an impossible shot to the green. If he played it safe, he would probably bogey the hole, if not worse. But Tiger gambled. He used a seven iron and hit a shot that curved nearly ninety degrees in the air. As everyone watched in astonishment, the ball came to a stop just off the green. It was an incredible approach, and enabled Tiger to two-putt and save par. It also allowed him to come in with a 34, 2-under-par, for the front nine. Huston still held the lead, but Tiger was getting close.

Tiger parred the first three holes on the back nine, then came to the 485-yard, par-5 thirteenth. Once again he blasted a drive well over 300 yards and straight down the fairway. His next shot was an eight iron that took the ball onto the green within twenty feet of the cup. Once again he showed a deft touch with his putter, sinking the ball for another eagle. That shot put him into the lead for the first time. John Huston, playing in the twosome behind Tiger, self-destructed on the thirteenth. He took a disastrous ten to put himself right out of contention.

Tiger coasted home with birdies on fourteen and fifteen, pars the rest of the way. He finished the round with the tournament's best score, a 66, and had vaulted out into a three-stroke lead over Scotland's Colin Montgomerie and a four-shot margin over Italy's Constantino Rocca. To show further how focused Tiger was, he didn't report to the press tent for the post-round news conference.

He immediately went out to the driving range to hit some more balls. Later, he would take some heat for this, but there were just twenty minutes of daylight left, and Tiger didn't want to break his post-round routine.

The second round also produced some interesting surprises. Among the golfers who didn't make the cut (didn't shoot below 150 and could not continue into the final rounds) were defending champ Faldo, Greg Norman, and Phil Mickelson—three players that a number of experts had picked to win. And the most pleasant surprise, besides Tiger's great spurt, was that six-time winner Jack Nicklaus had come in at 77-70—147, and fans would get the chance to see the legendary champion play the final thirty-six holes one more time.

But Tiger was still the main focus. He was playing with verve and confidence now, his 40 on the front nine on Thursday all but forgotten. In fact, he had played the last twenty-seven holes (not counting the first-round front nine) 12 under par with just a single bogey. In other words, he was playing nearly letter-perfect golf.

"He has the ability to do that," said Jack Nicklaus, referring to Tiger's assault on par. "That's why this young man is so special. If he's playing well, the golf course becomes nothing." Then Nicklaus added, "He's playing a game we're not familiar with."

Colin Montgomerie, who jumped into second place with a fine round of 67, said he had a chance to win if . . .

"Sure, I can win here," Montgomerie told reporters. "But it depends a lot on how Mr. Woods fares. The way he's playing, this course tends to suit him more than anyone else. If he decides to continue to do what he's doing, more credit to him and I'll shake his hand.

"At the same time, there's more to it than hitting the ball a long way. And the pressure is mounting more and more. I've got a lot more experience in major golf than he has. Hopefully, I can prove that through the weekend."

Though the words were mixed, his fellow pros seemed to be learning quickly that if Tiger is playing at the top of his game, no one can stop him. As Montgomerie concluded, "I'm playing the golf course right now and [Tiger] is playing his own ball. On the drives, I *wish* I was playing his ball. I'm looking foward to the challenge. I've got nothing to lose."

No wonder the other golfers wanted to play Tiger's ball on the drives. In the second round alone he averaged an incredible 336.5 yards per drive. That seemed nearly impossible, that a golfer with Tiger's slim build could have that kind of power. As one writer put it, he "hit drives to places no one had ever hit the ball before."

But that wasn't all. During the second round Tiger missed only one fairway all day, and needed just twenty-nine putts to complete the eighteen holes.

"I felt very comfortable with my game [today]," Tiger said. "I was very relaxed and patient. My strategy is to just drive the ball well on the par-5s. If I drive the ball well, I should reach all the par-5s in two."

As for his goal the final two rounds, that remained the same as it had been before the tournament began.

"This is what I came here to do, to try to win the tournament," Tiger said. "That's my main goal. To have a lead now, it's nice, but it's only the halfway point. I need to go out and shoot a low round tomorrow to put myself in a good position for Sunday."

Tiger was never one to rest on his laurels, not when there was more golf to be played. Never, in his entire career, had he become the least bit complacent. He wasn't about to start now, not with a three-stroke lead in the Masters.

On Saturday, the galleries continued to swell and the excitement continued to build. Could Tiger keep playing as if he were in another world? Or would one of the fine pros within striking distance be able to muster a run and challenge for the lead before the final round? It didn't take long for both those questions to be answered.

Tiger simply went out and overwhelmed the course again. While all those close to him seemed to falter, Tiger, if anything, got better. He shot a bogey-less round, going out in 32 on the front nine, and coming in with a 33 on the back nine for a tournament low 65. At the end of three rounds he was at 201, tying Raymond Floyd's mark for low score after three that was set back in 1976. Better yet, he now had what seemed like an insurmountable, record nine-stroke lead over Rocca and the rest of the field.

It almost seemed as if Tiger was playing a separate tournament. He was nine up on everyone else. Yet there were 16 golfers within seven strokes of one another between 210 and 217. When someone asked Colin Montgomerie, who had faded to 213, if anyone could catch Tiger, he said,

"There is no chance—no human chance possible—that Tiger Woods is going to lose this tournament. No way."

Then one reporter reminded Montgomerie that Greg Norman had lost a six-stroke lead to Nick Faldo in the final round the year before. Montgomerie just laughed.

"What makes you say that?" he snapped. "Have you been away? This is different. This is very different. Faldo is not second . . . and Greg Norman is not Tiger Woods."

The respect for Tiger among his fellow pros was obviously growing quickly. Paul Stankowski, who was at 211, said flatly, "Tomorrow there is no chance unless I shoot 57."

Even Tiger seemed a bit surprised that no other golfer had stepped up to challenge him.

"I told my pop before I left someone was going to make a run," he explained. "I'm a little surprised no one has made a run. But the tournament isn't over yet."

In the eyes of most, it was over. As Davis Love III

explained, "Everybody was trying to birdie every hole to try to catch up to him. That's a difficult way to play."

Even Tiger seemed to be thinking of victory, and what it ultimately would mean to him. These were things not usually said until after a tournament was won. But in his own mind, he must have known no one could possibly catch him, barring some kind of freak injury.

"[Winning] means a lot for a number of reasons," he said. "I would become the youngest to ever win, and more important, in my estimation, it will open up a lot of doors and draw a lot of people into golf who never thought of playing the game.

"On this kind of stage, this could do a lot for the game as far as minority golf is concerned."

Tiger was also asked what it would mean to be the first player of mixed race to win the Masters.

"It means that no one else has ever accomplished it who played the game. That means a lot to me. African-American players like Elder and Sifford will probably be going through several emotions. One, I'm sure they wish it could have been them. I love those guys to death and they love me, and I know they are very proud of what I've done so far."

It was apparent that Tiger was an athlete who thought about a lot more than himself. That, too, was extremely refreshing in view of the many me-only athletes performing these days. And Tiger was also an athlete who seemed to be revolutionizing his sport. Tom Kite, who shot a 66 in the third round and was 11 back at 212, made an interesting comparison.

"You know what Tiger has that is similar to what Jack [Nicklaus] had when he came on tour in the 60s? It's that he's way out in front of everybody else. It took nearly thirty years for everybody to catch up to what Jack was doing at the time. Well, this is the next generation, and Tiger's coming in and is leapfrogging the rest of the field."

But perhaps it was veteran pro Ben Crenshaw who said it best. Crenshaw grew up in golf's old tradition, where there were a few great players like Ben Hogan and Sam Snead, then Palmer and Nicklaus. As he left the Augusta National on Saturday night, following the third round of play, Crenshaw said a few simple words that told the whole story of Tiger Woods.

"Something's changing," Crenshaw said. "Something is about to pass."

Chapter 12

The Masters—Part Three

The fourth and final round of the Masters was played on Sunday, April 13. People were quick to point out an added significance to that day. On April 15, 1947, Jackie Robinson became the first African-American to play major league baseball. The baseball world, as well as many other venues, were already planning commemorative celebrations to mark the 50th anniversary of that day. And here was Tiger Woods, on the brink of becoming the first man of mixed race to win a major golf tournament.

Unlike many of today's athletes, Tiger was well aware of the significance of what he was about to do, and that it coincided with the 50th anniversary of Robinson's achievement. He also knew how much a victory would mean to the African-American golfers who came before. Lee Elder, the first black man to play in a Masters in 1975, talked about his feelings before the final round.

"I'm just so elated," Elder said. "Here we're going to have a black champion, and that's something that certainly makes my heart feel very warm. It gives me a lot of satisfaction because it means a lot for minorities. This is going to have a big impact on what will happen in the future.

"In those earlier years, I don't think [Tiger] would have been accepted like this. I don't think the world was ready to accept a black golf champion with open arms. I know what we went through, just playing. In '75, [Tiger] probably would have needed armed guards to get to the first tee.

"But today, things have changed."

When Elder approached Tiger to wish him luck just before he teed off to start the final round, the younger man was touched.

"That really reinforced what I had to accomplish," Tiger said. "He was the first. It was because of people like him that I was able to turn pro, to get this opportunity."

Tiger also went out on the course thinking about the words his father had spoken to him the night before.

"This is probably going to be one of the toughest rounds you've ever played in your life," Mr. Woods told his son. "But if you be yourself, it could be the most rewarding round you've ever played in your life."

On the golf course the crowds thronged around Tiger, who was paired with Constantino Rocca, the man who was nine shots behind. But the only competition in the final round would be between Tiger and the golf course. The outcome was never in doubt. One writer called Tiger's final eighteen-hole round a coronation. The new King of Golf had arrived.

That didn't mean that Tiger played soft or conservative. He attacked the Augusta National just as he had during the first three rounds. He didn't want to back in to the title with a mediocre round. His first tee shot was a rocket into the wind that went well up the fairway and to the left of a sand trap. His next shot was on the green, and he two-putted for a par.

"That was big," he said, "to settle down like that with two good shots and a solid par."

When Tiger birdied the second hole it looked as if he was on his way. Those scrambling behind him knew immediately there wasn't going **to** be any kind of total collapse. His first bogey in 37 holes came on the fifth and dropped his lead over Rocca and Tom Watson to eight strokes. But that was as close as anyone would get. After another bogey on seven, Tiger began playing errorless golf once again.

He played the front nine in 36, right on par. But as had been the case in the three previous rounds, the back nine was where he made his living. Brimming with confidence, he birdied the eleventh, thirteenth, and fourteenth to go 3 under par and increase his lead. When he parred the sixteenth with a beautiful curving putt and a tap-in, he finally breathed easier. He knew what everyone else had known since the second round. He had it won.

"After that," he said, "I knew I could bogey in and win."

He was so far ahead he probably could have won it with a pool cue. But as Tiger approached the eighteenth tee to another thunderous ovation, there was one other thing he wanted to achieve. A par at eighteen would give him a final score of 270, breaking the Masters record of 271 shared by Nicklaus and Raymond Floyd.

As he got set to hit, a nearby photographer clicked his shutter twice on his backswing. Tiger flinched slightly and hooked his drive way left. The gallery had to clear a path for his second shot. Still not losing his cool, he calmly hit yet another wedge shot onto the green. He then made the traditional walk up the last part of the fairway to the green. It was a walk many Masters champions had taken before. All had described it as one of the most satifying walks in golf, the crowd applauding and cheering the new champion, a moment to savor forever. Tiger smiled every step of the way.

His putt for birdie rolled about five feet past the cup. But he still had one more chance for a par and the record. He lined it up carefully, stood over the ball for a few seconds as the crowd hushed in absolute silence. Then he stroked it. The ball rolled in! The huge crowd erupted in yet another thunderous roar as Tiger punched the air with his trademark uppercut. He had shot a final round 69 to win the Masters by a record twelve strokes over runner-up Tom Kite.

Tiger walked quickly from the green and into the crowd. He made a beeline for his father. The two men embraced for what seemed like an eternity as the television camera caught an emotional moment that saw the tears flow freely. All their work over so many years. Everything they had done to prepare for this moment had been worth it. Then Tiger transferred the hug to his mother. Finally, all three of them hugged.

On his way to the clubhouse for a television interview, Tiger again spotted Lee Elder. The young champion put a giant bear hug on Elder and whispered in his ear, "Thanks for making this possible." Now it was Elder who couldn't hold back the tears.

What Tiger had done was truly remarkable, and would take a few days to really sink in. His 270 total score and twelve-stroke victory margin were both records. The old record was a nine-stroke margin by Nicklaus back in 1965. At age twenty-one, Tiger was the youngest golfer ever to win the Masters. The old mark belonged to Spain's Seve Ballesteros, who was twenty-three in 1980.

And, of course, his mixed heritage made him both the first African-American and first Asian to win both the Masters and one of the four "majors." In addition, it was his fourth victory in just fifteen PGA tournaments since turning pro. He also had a tie for second, two thirds and nine top-tens in those fifteen tournaments. There had never been a start like that in golf history.

Then the accolades began to come. One of the first came from President Bill Clinton, shortly after Tiger holed his final putt. The President called from the White House.

"He just said he was proud of the way I played," Tiger said. "He said he watched the entire tournament because he's been laid up with a bum knee. He also said the best shot he saw all week was the shot of me hugging my dad."

Then Tiger talked about his own thoughts. "This is something I've always dreamt of," he said. "I was able to [win the tournament]. It means a lot to myself and my family.

"It was a pretty amazing week. I've never played an entire tournament with my 'A' game, and this was pretty close. Excluding the first nine holes, this was my 'A' game. But more than anything else, I'm relieved that it's over. Every time, I hug my mom or pop after it's over. It's just great for me to share it with them. That's special."

The reaction from everyone else was just as emphatic. Jack Nicklaus, one of Tiger's earliest and most vocal boosters, repeated an earlier prediction.

"Arnold [Palmer] and I both agree," Nicklaus said, "that you can take his Masters (four) and my Masters (six), add them together, and this kid should win more than that."

Then Nicklaus added, "[Tiger's] out there playing another game on a golf course he is going to own for a long time. I don't think I want to go back out and be twenty-one and compete against him."

At the official ceremony, last year's winner, Nick Faldo, slipped the traditional green jacket over Tiger's shoulders. Tiger's smile spoke volumes, as the jacket was a perfect fit. Even his fellow pros, the ones he had humbled, applauded and congratulated him.

Jasper Parnevik, who finished nineteen shots behind Tiger, said that "unless they build Tiger tees about fifty yards back, he's going to win the next twenty of these."

Paul Azinger, who was in contention briefly at the outset, noted that Tiger "never had a mental lapse," adding "The bigger the event, the higher he'll raise the bar. He's Michael Jordan in long pants."

And Charlie Sifford, one of the first black pros to play on the PGA circuit, was also overwhelmed by the spectacle. At age seventy-four, Sifford watched the tournament from his home.

"This is a wonderful thing for golf," Sifford said, "never mind the racial thing. This is just a kid who's doing what I wanted to do, but never had the chance to do."

Tiger Woods not only had the chance. He made the most of it with one of the most dominating performances in golfing history.

Chapter 13

What Comes Next

When an athlete like Tiger Woods comes along, one whose achievements, charisma, and popularity transcend his sport, he often finds himself pulled in several directions at once. After his win in the Masters, Tiger had achieved that special, elevated status. The fact that he was so often equated with basketball's Michael Jordan was no accident. Jordan was one of the few athletes who had not only survived, but prospered in that lofty position.

Jordan has remained at the top of his sport for a dozen years, even after sitting out nearly two seasons when he played minor league baseball. In 1997, at age thirty-four, he is still widely considered not only the best player in the NBA, but the greatest of all time. Besides basketball, Jordan has a slew of commercial endeavors, has recently made a feature film for kids, *Space Jam*, and led his team, the Chicago Bulls, into contention for another NBA championship.

In some ways, however, the pressure on Tiger Woods could turn out to be even greater. His triumph at the Masters was the most watched golf tournament ever. Sunday's final round earned a 15.8 rating, beating every other weekend program with the exception of *60 Minutes*.

"The traditional golf audience at its peak is eight or nine rating points," said David Poltrack, CBS's chief ratings analyst. "Almost half of this Masters' audience was nontraditional [golf fans]."

Poltrack added that there hadn't been an impact on the ratings like that since the Olympic skating controversy between Tonya Harding and Nancy Kerrigan. But it was also said that golf ratings would only stay that high if Tiger was in contention to win.

That said two things. A huge number of people now knew the story of Tiger Woods, had seen his skills, his face, his smile, his emotional moment with his parents. That made Tiger a potentially huge personality, one with enormous marketing potential. The day after the Masters, his management firm reported that prospective business deals were pouring into their office at the incredible rate of one per minute! People were willing to spend millions of dollars just to get Tiger Woods to endorse their products.

"Tiger's potential is unlimited, tens of millions of dollars a year, whatever he wants to make," said

Frank Vuono, of Integrated Sports International, a sports marketing and licensing firm.

So far as marketing is concerned, it would seem that Tiger has his pick. He has said in the past that he didn't want to be king of the endorsers. His two contracts, with Nike and Titleist, as well as his potential golf earnings, could well give him and his family all the money they need for the rest of their lives. How much additional endorsing and marketing they choose to do will be strictly up to them.

The other truth generated by the high television ratings for the Masters made another thing very clear. To stay at the top, Tiger Woods has to keep winning. There is no reason to believe that his skills will deteriorate if he continues along the same route he has come. To the contrary, his skills could well improve as he grows older and stronger. He has the potential to dominate the game as no player before him.

As soon as he won the Masters, there was talk of the possibility of a Grand Slam. The Grand Slam would consist of winning all four majors—Masters, U.S. Open, British Open, and PGA Tournament—in the same year. The Grand Slam has been done only once, and even then it wasn't quite the same.

That was in 1930, when the legendary Bobby Jones won four majors. But Jones was an amateur. His Grand Slam consisted of the U.S. Open, U.S. Amateur, British Open, and British Amateur. The Masters wasn't played then, and the PGA Tournament was not open to amateurs. So no modern player has ever done it.

In fact, no player since Jack Nicklaus in 1972 has ever won the first two legs of the Slam. But the consensus seems to be that Tiger has a chance. Even he admitted it was possible.

"Whether it's realistic or not, I couldn't really tell you," he said to a question that would be asked of him many times. "But I think it can be done. If you think about it, let's say, for example, Phil Mickelson won four times last year. Well, if you win the right tournaments four times, then you have the Slam.

"It's difficult to win, though, because these are the majors. These are the best players in the world under the most extreme conditions and circumstances. But I think if you peak at the right times—a lot like what [Jack] Nicklaus used to do—and have a lot of luck on your side, it can be done."

Jerry Pate, the 1976 U.S. Open champion, pointed out that all four golf courses where the majors will be played in 1997 are made for Tiger's long game. And someone else noted that no one had ever won three straight U.S. Junior amateur titles before Woods, no one had won three straight U.S. Amateur titles before Woods, and no one had ever won the Masters at age twenty-one before Tiger Woods. And no one had ever averaged 328 yards off the tee for the Masters before Tiger.

Jack Nicklaus, a man who knows the game from experience and golf courses because he designs them, is another who feels Tiger has a chance.

"It's not very likely, but it's possible," Nicklaus said. "When you're climbing a mountain, it's easier to climb when you're young. But let's take it one round at a time."

The U.S. Open is the next major, in June. Should Tiger win there, Tigermania, as the frenzy has been dubbed, would increase even more. But even if Tiger doesn't make the Grand Slam, it's very conceivable that he will win a number of additional tournaments this year. Remember, he said long ago that golf was like a drug to him, an addiction, something he needs. There is very little doubt that he will continue to work on his game with the same intensity he has shown since the age of two.

Then there is the responsibility that goes with being the most popular figure in his sport, as well as a man of mixed heritage. That seems to be something Tiger is already addressing. The Tiger Woods Foundation is now a reality. Tiger will be working to expose inner-city kids to golf through clinics he will host throughout the PGA Tour season. He has scheduled clinics in many cities, starting with Dallas, just a month after the Masters.

The clinics are just one-day events. But Tiger's father has said that one of the primary objectives with the Woods Foundation is to establish follow-up programs to the clinics, a task Earl Woods is coordinating with the National Minority Golf Foundation.

"What golf needs to do is get an organized approach in each community and get the country clubs and golf courses in that community to support the programs," Mr. Woods explained. "They need to assure that kids have affordable places to practice and play, make the game available and make it fun."

Tiger feels that his young age will help him get the message across.

"I'm in a very unique position, where a lot of kids look up to me just because I'm around their age group," he said. "They look up to me in a role-model sense. I think winning [the Masters] is going to do a lot for the game of golf. A lot of kids will start playing it now, and over time, hopefully, I'll be around to see the fruits."

As time passes and his popularity increases, Tiger will be forced to make decisions regarding his time. Whenever he turns down a request to attend a charity event, he will be criticized. That, however, isn't really fair. Bill Dickey, president of the National Minority Junior Golf Scholarship Association, feels Tiger must simply set his priorities and keep them.

"The biggest thing for Tiger to do is enjoy the game, play well, and split up his time where he can be most effective," Dickey said. "We're just thrilled to death that Tiger is doing what we knew he could."

Dickey's Association has awarded $330,000 in scholarships to 286 colleges and college-bound minority golfers since 1983. He says, however, that there was a time when he had to shout for attention. Now the phone is ringing off the hook with people interested in minority golf programs.

"Just like there are kids who want to be like Mike (Michael Jordan)," Dickey said, "there are kids who want to be like Tiger. What we have to do is find a way to give them that opportunity."

So Tiger's impact is already being felt at several levels. The PGA Tour expects a big increase in revenues, both from television rights and attendance at tournaments, and that is due to a huge extent to the emergence of Tiger Woods.

So right now Tiger Woods is sitting on top of the world. His impact on the world of sports and the world of golf has been enormous. His talent, personality, and maturity should allow him to remain on top—as both a golfer and a celebrity—for many years to come.

One of his fellow pros, Nick Price, put things in perspective when he said, soon after the Masters, "Nine months doesn't make a career. [Tiger] has got a long way to go."

Price's remarks weren't meant to be derogatory. They were simply realistic. Sports has seen many one-shot wonders, athletes who flared brightly for a short time, then somehow lost the magic and never quite found it again. That will continue to be a question until Tiger Woods proves it's no longer relevant. That is entirely up to him.

"I know my goal is to obviously be the best player in the world," Tiger has said. "I know that's a very lofty goal, but if I try to accomplish that goal and I do, great. If I don't, I tried. I expect nothing but the best for myself."

Those are the words of a young man who has everything together. And as he said once before, when it really comes down to it, "I'm the one who has to make the shot. Me. Alone."

About the Author

Bill Gutman has been a free-lance writer for more than twenty years. In that time he has written well over 125 books for children and adults, many of which are about sports. He has written profiles and biographies of many sports stars from both past and present, as well as writing about all the major sports, and some lesser ones as well. Aside from biographies, his sports books include histories, "how-to" instructionals, and sports fiction. He is the author of Archway's *Sports Illustrated* series, biographies of Bo Jackson, Michael Jordan, Shaquille O'Neal, and Grant Hill, as well as *NBA High-Flyers*, profiles of top NBA stars. All are available from Archway Paperbacks. Mr. Gutman currently lives in Dover Plains, New York, with his wife and family.